HAGTALE

HAGTALE

Sally O'Reilly

A Macbeth Origin Story

SCRIBE
Melbourne | London | Minneapolis

Scribe Publications
18–20 Edward St, Brunswick, Victoria 3056, Australia
2 John St, Clerkenwell, London, WC1N 2ES, United Kingdom
3754 Pleasant Ave, Suite 223w, Minneapolis, Minnesota 55409, USA

Published by Scribe 2025

Copyright © Sally O'Reilly 2025

The publisher expressly prohibits the use of *Hagtale* in connection with the development of any software program, including, without limitation, training a machine-learning or generative artificial intelligence (AI) system.

All rights reserved, including those for text and data mining, AI training, and similar technologies. Without limiting the rights under copyright reserved above, no part of this publication may be reproduced, stored in or introduced into a retrieval system, or transmitted, in any form or by any means (electronic, mechanical, photocopying, recording or otherwise) without the prior written permission of the publishers of this book.

The moral rights of the author have been asserted.

Typeset in Garamond Premier Pro by the publishers

Printed and bound in the UK by CPI Group (UK) Ltd, Croydon CR0 4YY

Scribe is committed to the sustainable use of natural resources and the use of paper products made responsibly from those resources.

978 1 761381 43 0 (Australian edition)
978 1 917189 08 8 (UK edition)
978 1 761386 55 8 (ebook)

Catalogue records for this book are available from the National Library of Australia and the British Library.

scribepublications.com.au
scribepublications.co.uk
scribepublications.com

To Declan

Prologue

Prologue

Tangled by the root into the living ground, gnarled and twisted, formed into giant and massy shape by rain and sun and passing seasons, the dark trees listen. Beyond the steeply clustered forest, the land rolls upward, to the squat outline of the castle. The forest stills itself, a silence unknown in all its green and gold and burgeoning summers, its snowbound winters. No sound, no movement; nothing breathes. Far off the castle seethes, giving up laments and death-cries.

Birnam Wood has lived here for ten thousand years, tranquil for long tracts of time. But this has changed. There has been felling, burning, robbing. Men have left it wounded and in pain, murdering its sapwood before slaying their own kind. The ancient forest will rise and show its power. Now, there's whispering and stirring, from branch to wormy soil. Leaves turn to face the black shape on the hill. Roots unsnarl themselves from their moist and rotted home, pulling upward towards the surface. High above, the topmost branches are pointing the same way. The great wood moves with vegetable sureness: broad trunks creak, wild arms shuck off leaves and nests. Gradually, the sound of whispering grows louder. The trees inch forward, over startled ground, their creeping roots like grasping fingers.

I
MIDLOTHIAN, 1354

Rowan rests on his spade and considers the abbey garden. It's high summer, and it seems to him a veritable Eden, with its stone walls and orderly, rectangular plan. Each quarter is laid out for a different purpose: flowers, vegetables, herbs, and scythe-mown grass, where daisies and periwinkles grow. At its centre is a fountain, its gentle plashing mingling with the sound of birdsong. Beyond the walls lies the orchard, also laid out in perfect symmetry, where there are fruit trees and beehives. The contemplation of this garden, beautiful as well as practical, is one of the few remaining pleasures of his life. He feels blessed by its sheer variety and looks around him at the flowers: lady's bedstraw, dancing violets, scarlet roses, scented lavender. Colours shift and dazzle. For the last few months, he has come here every morning, and as spring unfurled each flower, the trees gave out their blossoms and put on tender, translucent leaves, and the bees came to suck, their drunken buzzing louder every day. Now, nature has reached its zenith, and God's munificence is all around him. As the garden has given forth its bounty, he has recovered too, and now he can almost fancy that he's regained his strength. Even though the hearing in one ear has gone, and he still has that racking pain, which visits him most days, like the knowledge of mortality, streaking from one joint to another, then to his belly, then his head. He knows of no one else who lived after catching the pestilence, and is duly grateful for every breath he takes. But he is not the man he was. The plague still inhabits him, or its ghost does. Inside the monastery, in the cold sequestered half-light, he feels it sorely, this depletion, whereas in the sunlit garden he feels more like his former self.

Nothing afflicts him more acutely than working in the scriptorium, where he used to sit for hour after hour, on a hard stool, with the goose-quill clenched between his fingers. There was a time when he was perfectly happy thus occupied and willingly ignored its physical discomforts. Because, as he worked there, copying the words of those who'd gone before, his mind was filled with visions: of kingship, heroism, pageantry, and knighthood; of saintly interventions and noble pilgrimages.

Rowan has always been amenable, accommodating, a gentle, thoughtful man. Perhaps this has its roots in his being a stranger here — his family are from Tyrconnell in Ulster, and when he was a boy, he had spoken the language of that region. That child has gone now, but the words of his homeland and their particular diction have stayed with him, similar, but different, to the Gaelic they speak here in Midlothian. He was hardly more than a boy when he entered the priory, and his home is the Church, his lingua franca Latin, which he chants throughout the day. So there is little to see or hear in Rowan that would mark him out as different from his fellow cloisterers. The differences are within: his memory, the songs that ripple through his mind when he is digging cabbages, and his interest in old tongues, which are no longer spoken.

There is the lost Irish boy, and there is the lost Rowan from before the pestilence. That was when he saw Hell, or something like it, and was changed, for good or ill. Once, he liked nothing better than to dip his quill into black ink, and form neat letters on the parchment, each flowing into the other, proceeding in perfect order across the velvet softness of the page. Yet now, this task has lost its savour. The scriptorium is no longer a place of sanctuary — it feels like a prison. The work is servitude and the very thought of it fills him with gloom: the smell of iron gall, the tall north-facing window, and the crouched forms of his fellow scribes. These days, he prefers to work outdoors, under the open sky, with a breeze upon his cheek. Nothing that a man can make will ever rival nature. He would rather grow cabbages and roses than crouch over a lectern. Besides, the gardener is essential, whereas a scholar is merely useful. If the land fails, men starve. If books were gone, humans would endure, carrying stories in their heads.

The remoteness of the priory's location was a blessing during the pestilence; lives were lost, but other monasteries suffered more acutely. Since the plague time, those more ambitious than Rowan have had their own preoccupations, leaving him to his digging and weeding. A kind of normality has been established, with perhaps half the number of monks that there once were, and there's a sense of being forgotten, that the great world is going about its business oblivious to the existence of this small mountain haven. The Maker sees everything, and every human soul: this backwater is as dear to him as St Peter's church at Rome. Or so Rowan conceives it, but he is suited to a quiet life. However, the new prior is a great reformer, and Rowan knows that his attention must soon turn to the scriptorium and its contribution to the house.

The call comes before too long. He waits patiently in the prior's study, watching while Father Andrew finishes a letter. Why he has been summoned, he doesn't know. But he is uneasy; the prior's plans rarely bode well for his inferiors. As soon as he took charge, he began ordering needless and costly 'improvements' to be made: the rood screen must be freshly gilded, and new fish-stews stocked with Flemish carp. Yet, thinks Rowan, there is no reason to suppose that such changes enhance the monks' prayers on behalf of the populace or render their collective piety more profound.

Father Andrew is a smiler, a giggler, a fellow always in good humour. He is polite, thoughtful, ready to offer praise.

Always giving way to others in a debate, never pushing himself forward. Faultless, so it seems, in his modest sense of what is mete and proper, happy in his station. So it is one of the great mysteries of the universe that he has ascended so fast, while other men have fallen out of favour. After the pestilence, which rapidly saw off old Father Paul, and following that his successor, Father Simon, there were still candidates who had been longer at the priory, who were more obvious replacements.

Rowan must set such thoughts aside. Father Andrew's elevation to prior must be the Will of God. He sends up a prayer, a fragmentary obeisance. God's Will Be Done. And it is done. One cannot hope to know the purpose.

'You've been spending your time digging the garden, so I hear,' says Father Andrew, with his charming smile.

'Indeed, yes, Reverend Father. But I hope not more time than I should. After all, it is part of our calling. There's no question of my neglecting my spiritual life.'

'Oh quite, quite! I am full of admiration for your outdoor work, and no one doubts your piety, no, not at all. But equally —' (here the prior pauses not to smile exactly, but to fix Rowan with a look of active beneficence) '— it is not only a matter of praying and working in the garden, is it? If I may be so bold — and taking nothing away from the benefits of *earthly toil* — there is particular work to be done in the scriptorium. Particular and of great value. And you, among all the brethren, have a gift for this work.

Which should not be neglected. Remember the parable of the talents.' So much good will is aimed at Rowan that he feels increasingly uneasy.

'Thank you for your kind words, Reverend Father, but I do fear that you overstate my skill. I have a neat hand,' he says. 'Which is hardly the most unusual of gifts. And gardening is useful to my brothers in the scriptorium, who are more suited to that sort of work. The iris root makes a decent ink, for instance, as well as having a pleasant smell.'

'You are too modest! Your mind is clear, just as your hand is steady.' The prior smiles winningly, and Rowan feels compelled to smile himself. Yet what does the prior know of clear minds? His own is cluttered with thoughts of his advancement.

'Working the soil has aided my convalescence. I hope that by continuing to spend time among the plants and flowers, I might improve still further, and then I can return to my former work fully restored.'

'This convalescence, as you call it, has been going on for some time. And the world continues on its way. There are tasks which we, in our diminished state, must address, with fewer brethren to choose from.'

'Forgive me, Reverend Father, but I am not entirely sure which tasks you are referring to.'

'The late pestilence has dealt us a mortal blow,' says the prior. 'Other monasteries too — whole cities. The tales that have come from Stirling are beyond belief. We are at the mercy of whomever wishes to overwhelm us.'

'*Does* anyone wish to do such a thing?'

Frowning, Father Andrew looks out of the window, at the lush green orchard and the misted blue of the distant mountains. 'Brother Rowan, you are a kindly fellow, but perhaps naïve. The world beyond these walls is a ruthless one. The English are laying claim to our lands, and they wish to populate our past as well. There has been much disputation over Scotland, as you are aware, and what we need now are detailed records of lineages and genealogy. Kept here, where they belong. Alba's king-line reaches back to the great warriors of Ireland. But the stories of our heroes have been stolen from us, and are held in London, where they may easily be destroyed. If we manage to compile a decent chronicle, it will bring this monastery great renown.'

These are not matters to which Rowan has given much thought. 'That is all most interesting, Reverend Father. Yet, forgive me, I am not sure how this relates to my labours.'

'Weren't you engaged in writing about our forebears before you were struck down? I thought the late prior commissioned a history of the Scottish kings?'

'After a fashion. I would not make any great claims for it ... I made a fair copy from various fragments. What I made was itself a fragment, I'm afraid. There is not much to see.'

'Yes, exactly, that is what I have been looking at. Your discoveries were impressive, and your work on them exemplary. This start makes you the ideal man. Brother

Rowan, let me make myself quite plain. I have a job for you. I'd like you to make a journey.'

'A journey? Really? Where to?' Rowan's mind reels at the prospect. He has lived here for twenty years and more and has not contemplated leaving.

'Not so very far. I'm not asking you to travel to Avignon or Rome! Merely to a place where you might consult documents that record the lives of certain Scottish kings, whose names are missing from the present record. And thus complete the work which you have lately undertaken.'

Rowan is used to being compliant. His greatest wish is for a quiet life, and so the last thing he wants to do is refuse outright to obey his prior. Yet he is not only baffled but incredulous, and struggles to understand what is being asked of him. 'I did some work before the pestilence and have only the dimmest recollection of its nature. It would not be easy to resume. Indeed, it would not be a resumption, but a new beginning.'

Father Andrew purses his lips and shakes his head. 'We simply need a man who knows his way around an archive, can make a good copy, and bring it back to me. But in so doing, you will provide me with a jewel, with invaluable knowledge. Saint Medard's monastery has been standing empty for many years. When the plague struck, not a soul survived. Its library is said to contain many unique and valuable texts, and these are at risk of destruction. The abbey is on the shores of a loch, and it has been flooded on several occasions. There may not be much time.'

'That is ... I am astonished, Reverend Father.'

'Come now, there is no need to look so glum! It's a journey of two hundred miles, so I am told. We must go there and investigate, see what can be found.'

'Shall you be travelling with me?'

'No, no, I was meaning "we" the monastery, the collective body, the brethren, represented by yourself. But I'm not expecting you to go alone. You will need assistance and protection. Brother Kenneth will accompany you. He is a strong fellow and will be a sturdy and loyal companion.'

Rowan stares at the prior in alarm. 'Reverend Father, please, I beg you to reconsider ... I can scarcely rise each day, such is the tiredness in my bones. I am partly deaf. I am exhausted after a morning's digging ...'

Father Andrew smiles patiently. 'Yet you say the garden restores you.'

'Gardening is not to be compared to a journey such as this. It lightens the spirit. Did not God Himself create a garden, before all else? One can be close to Him through the practice of horticulture. And does not St Benedict enjoin us to cultivate a garden?' He is babbling like a fool.

The prior is implacable. 'Travelling will renew your spirits,' he says. 'You will be on the open road, in the midst of nature's grandeur, the glories of Creation.'

'Perhaps in three months. I have made much progress and will be stronger then.'

'Time is of the essence, and we must accomplish this as soon as possible. I can provide you with some information about the route, and there is a former associate of mine in Edinburgh who can advise you further. He was once a member of the Order, though he has now left and works as an independent scholar, so I understand.'

'But, Reverend Father, this is work for a team of scholars, not one man and his protector!'

'You know how we are placed. No other suitable men survive. It is not such a great ordeal. You will proceed from here to the North Road, and then I believe it's a day's ride to Edinburgh. There you will stay with the associate I mentioned, who is knowledgeable in these matters. And he will travel with you to the abbey.'

'What sort of matters, might I ask?'

'Ancient documents, arcane texts, the sort of knowledge one acquires through lengthy scholarship. Though Gervaise MacCrone himself is youthful. A brilliant man, an incomparable mind. A worthy addition to your party.'

'This is all rather sudden, and unexpected, and while I'm sure Brother Kenneth has some knowledge of the world, I have very little.'

'Let me put your mind at rest. I have every confidence in you. Otherwise, I would not give you this commission.'

'And how far is the abbey from Edinburgh?'

The prior flips his hands vaguely. 'Not too far, I don't think. Gervaise will be your guide.'

Rowan tries to envisage this: the distance, the uncertainty, the danger. His mind fills with a clamour of memories, shapes, and sounds from boyhood — inns, and wimpled wives, and shopfronts, and louts debating nonsense in the market square. He thinks of footpads, though he has never seen one. The room begins to shift and shimmer around him.

'Don't tell me that you aren't equal to this task. Nor is it an unusual or unreasonable request; you needn't look so crestfallen. Cloisterers are often sent on just such errands.'

'My main concern is —'

'Your poor health should not prevent you, for are you not called by God to do this? Shall you ignore the invitation of the Maker? Besides, it may be that a change of scene improves your spirits, and thus your physical condition.'

The afternoon sun slants pleasantly through the window of the prior's study, illuminating a flagon of red wine, which flashes like rubies. Two glasses are set beside it, and a plate of figs. Rowan has a vision of the journeys it has taken to furnish Father Andrew with these luxuries. He does not know much of the outside world, but what he does know fills him with trepidation. He thinks of the distant lands of which travellers have written, some nearly as hot as the fires of Hell, and those eastern realms where children fatten up their parents and ritually consume them. And the island that has two summers and two winters and is beset by flying dragons. Of course, there are no such dangers and privations in the north, only bitter cold and (presumably) a greater concentration of ravening wolves.

Father Andrew opens his writing desk as if about to begin some other business. 'As I say, there is no time to waste. Others may have a similar notion. Prepare to depart by the end of the week.'

Rowan can scarcely speak, such is his consternation. A perilous journey, on a dubious mission. Accompanied by Brother Kenneth! The man is the very pattern of virtue, piety, and industry — the mark of a recent convert. He has every virtue but humanity, every quality but kindness.

'Reverend Father, I really must ...'

'If you succeed in this, you will help establish Scotland's ancestral lineage despite the interference of Edward and his English lackeys. And by doing so, the name of this abbey will itself be glorified. There is nothing further to be said. God bless you, brother. And may He speed you on your way.'

II
THREE HUNDRED YEARS EARLIER

Snow is falling when she wakes. Sounds are muffled; the trees are stark black against the white. She shivers, aching with cold. The rough down on her body is soft and barely visible. Compared to the other beasts, she is bald and feeble. Only her long, matted hair resembles their warm coats. Why is she so cold? Where are the others? She sees herself riding on her mother's back, hands tangled in the soft curling wool beneath the bristles. Hunger gnaws her innards; she needs fresh meat. How is there food without the wolves?

She gets up and makes her way into the grieving woodland. There is a howling, far away, not a voice she knows. Turning away from the sound, she follows one of the tracks her mother showed her, until she comes to a frozen stream and a snow-banked oak tree. Breaking the ice, she laps at the water, gasping with the cold. She thinks of fish, the wider river near the seashore. Sniffing the air, she finds the track towards the sea, weaving between thick trees. Above the naked branches, dawn streaks grey and yellow.

There's birdsong, trembling, tumbling. The woodland thins; there is spiked grass and gusts of colder wind.

She follows the treeline down to the river. The water winds between the steep banks, glistening in the sun. High woods stand above the banks; beyond these are hunched mountains. She sees the fish; she tastes its flesh. Her mother would splash through water, seize the wriggling fish in her jaws. Carry it to the bank, its silver blotched with blood. Still throbbing as they ate. Following the memory, she makes her way to the water. She stares down at stones and seagrass. Before long, there's a dark shape moving beneath the surface. Wading in, she bends to catch it. She is slower than her mother. It's gone, she does not get a touch of it, yet even as she stands there, another fish bumps against her legs. She whirls round and falls into the freezing water. The shock drags a cry out of her, halfway to a howl, and she staggers to the shore, sight blurred, gasping sorely. The shape of Other Beast is there, further along the river, with his long threads reaching out into the water. Sometimes her mother would chase Other Beast away and take his catch. Now, it's the other way about; she might be prey. She goes limping and shivering back towards the trees, and tries to picture berries, the kinds that other creatures eat, and nests with eggs, but this is not the season.

Nothing is real but hunger. What might be food surrounds her: flying, crawling, calling. But all she can find to eat is earthworms. She gulps them down, slippery, writhing. There's an evil taste in her mouth, and her head is aching. She wanders among trees and snowy clearings. Sun and moon move slowly. The forest seethes with the unseen. Night creatures stalk her, whispering their ancient madness. Then she senses something — a presence. She blinks. There are three hooded figures at the edge of the clearing. Smelling the air, she cocks her head, puzzled by their scent.

III

Sitting in the cloister while Brother John Three trims his tonsure, Rowan watches Brother Kenneth undergoing the same procedure. By chance, they are sitting directly opposite one another. The two rows of seated monks and their barbers are silent. All he can hear is the sound of blade against scalp, the cooing of pigeons and the splashing water of the fountain. Kenneth is one of the new recruits they took in after the plague, when only fifteen monks were still living. The depletion of the population meant the usual requirements were relaxed, and there was less scrutiny of piety and suitability. Most of the new intake are loud, coltish lads, who must be fed between Matins and Terce, lest they overstuff themselves at dinner, and supervised in the dormitory for fear of diabolic lewdness. Kenneth is not like this. He seems to have been hewn, rather than born; his face is riven with deep lines, and his stance is upright, like something made from stone not skin and bone. There's an air of determination and certainty about him that fills Rowan with gloom. They have rarely spoken at length, but he knows Kenneth's story: he was once a soldier and had joined a Spanish crusade. The military life seems to have given him a lasting taste for discipline and orders. There is no doubt about his dedication to Our Lord — he's a passionate adherent to church ritual, punctilious in his observation.

Rowan reflects that Kenneth seems more certain about every aspect of his worship than he is himself about a single one. His excuse may be that the pestilence has made him doubtful, but a better Christian would accept that man cannot know God's will, and neither the number of deaths nor their nature are fit cause for despair.

Rowan should seek to emulate Kenneth, truly. He is the first to rise, the last to sleep, the first to fast, the last to break it. In the chapel, his voice, pure and plangent, rises above those of the other monks. Perhaps it's because he came to ordination later in life, having lived previously in the world; perhaps this makes him more readily observant, quicker to see the value of his calling. It's also possible that this feeling of difference, if not antipathy, is mutual. Even though Kenneth keeps to himself in general, he converses with the other monks more freely than he does with Rowan. *He smells the doubt on me*, thinks Rowan. *As dogs can smell a canker, so he can sense my moral failing.* But these thoughts are themselves impious.

Observing Kenneth's almost unworldly cleanliness, Rowan is aware of the soil under his fingernails, which he never seems able to shift, even after the most prolonged and vigorous handwashing. He watches as a lock of Kenneth's dark hair falls to the ground. He seems oblivious to all around him, keeping his eyes cast down, deep in contemplation. Rowan knows he should view his appointed companion with Christian charity, yet he cannot. The journey will be an ordeal in any case, but a more agreeable companion might at least have made the prospect a little less daunting.

He reflects on his ill-suitedness for the task. *I am not a learned man*, he thinks. The Reverend Father has mistaken dexterity for knowledge. Of course, he is aware of the basic truths all educated men must know. There are two spiritual states of man, Before Christ and After Christ, the earlier being unaware of Christ's Salvation, three states of religious law, seven ages of the world, and five modes of living, the first being bestial, natural, and ungovernable. Furthermore, there are seven types of person whose lives are deserving of a written record, and eight methods of recording time. But learned? No, he is not learned. He knows just enough to comprehend the vast reach of his ignorance.

As they leave the cloisters, he sees Kenneth walk out into the monastery gardens. Despite his misgivings, he must at least talk to the fellow. He catches up with Kenneth close to the wicket gate to the orchard. 'Brother Kenneth! I gather we are soon to be better acquainted. A challenging mission, I am sure you will agree.'

'We are entrusted with a great task,' says Kenneth, coolly.

'Indeed so. I only hope that I am equal to it.'

'God will give you strength.' Kenneth's smile is thin, perhaps also disapproving.

'Our quest is in His hands, of course.' Rowan sounds more pious than he feels.

'They have chosen our horses,' says Kenneth. 'The Reverend Father says we should ready ourselves for our departure — will you come with me to see them?' A show of friendliness, perhaps? But there is no warmth in this invitation.

They pass along the cloisters and passageways of the monastery, and cross the orchard, finally entering the dark, straw-smelling stable. There is silence except for the muffled sounds of horses munching hay and their hooves clunking as they shift in their stalls. The groom shows them their mounts. Rowan has been given a docile grey mare named Hestia, while Kenneth will ride Zeus, a tall dun cob. Who has named these beasts, wonders Rowan? Was it in jest? It seems odd that they will be riding horses with the nomenclature of pagan gods.

'They tell me you can handle a horse well,' says the stable boy to Kenneth.

'I ride well enough,' says Kenneth. 'I worked as a groom once.'

'I'm afraid I am a poor horseman,' says Rowan, giving Hestia an apple he was keeping in his pocket. He likes the touch of her soft lips against his palm. 'Nor have I ridden for some time — it was before I had the pestilence.'

'Let us try them out!' says Kenneth. Rowan had not expected this, but it seems churlish to demur.

The horses are saddled up and led out into the stableyard. The mounting block seems perilously high as Rowan climbs up, feeling old and heavy. Once there, the mare seems too far away, and he reaches out feebly while the stable boy holds her head. The only remedy seems to be to throw himself towards the saddle, and in doing so he almost overbalances, narrowly avoiding a tumble into the mud. But he manages to collect himself, grabs the reins, and forces his feet into the stirrups, sending a violent pain along his left leg in the process. Hestia stands patiently throughout, and he wonders what it is like to be this creature, with a metal bit across her tongue and a man's weight on her back. Meanwhile, Kenneth has nimbly mounted Zeus, who is tossing his head and swishing his tail.

'We're not off yet, hold your patience!' cries Kenneth. But even as he speaks, he touches the horse's sides with his heels and off they go, round and round the stableyard at a brisk trot, hardly slower than a canter. Rowan feels dizzy watching them. Merely sitting in the saddle is causing him significant discomfort. He cannot imagine how he will feel if they spend all day on horseback. Against his wishes, the grey lumbers after Zeus, and breaks into a slow trot. The yard and the clustered monastery buildings beyond revolve slowly as he bounces up and down on the hard saddle.

'Please!' he cries.

Kenneth overtakes him, and his own mount whinnies. Whether with anxiety or excitement or a mixture of the two, he cannot say, but Hestia speeds up; her gait changes and she begins to canter. Rowan grabs hold of her mane.

'Will someone stop this? I can't hold on!'

Kenneth rides alongside him, grabs the bridle, and the two riders slow down, finally coming to a standstill. 'These are both excellent beasts,' he says to the stable boy. He avoids looking at Rowan.

'A carriage may be preferable ...' says Rowan, hopelessly, as he slithers to the ground.

'There is no question of that,' says Kenneth. 'There is no road to speak of for much of the journey, no more than a mountain track.' He leaps from the saddle and hands the reins dismissively to the stable boy.

The weather has changed; black clouds have rolled in from the west. They hurry back to the stables with the horses just before the first raindrops fall. It's an almighty downpour, like the tumbling waters of a cataract. What will they do when they encounter such weather on the road? How shall he live, out in the world? Looking up at the raging sky, Rowan offers a mute prayer to the Blessed Virgin.

IV

For a while, she stands still, watching the three figures. She is trying to place their scent. Not plant, not fungi, not Beast, nor Other Beast, yet something like all three. Her fear tells her to turn and run, but she is curious. And she knows that she can't run as fast as usual, weak from those long days of starvation. She can hear the tree branches clacking in the cold sky, a weasel nosing though the undergrowth, the quiet slicking of a worm. The three figures make no sound at all.

Finally, one of the figures moves forward, over the shivering white ground, and she hears it speak.

'What is it made of?' Queerly, she understands this, though all she knows is wolf-tongue.

Another voice says: 'Mormaer blood.'

And a third. 'It's not their breed. Stark naked, and look how it moves.' It's an old woman's voice that speaks, cracked and dry.

'Unlearned in their ways,' says the first voice. 'A mongrel changeling.'

Something tightens in the air at these words. Sniffing, she tries to find a name for what has come. But there is only the scent of the three figures: of fish, of sour milk, of sweet old flesh.

'Unclaimed.' The third speaker. 'Untethered. It is wandering. It is empty. It is our vessel.'

The three figures move closer to her. She bares her teeth.

Their hoods diminish; they are revealed. The first speaker is aged, with a face fallen and riven, eyes scored and bloodshot. The second is younger, stout and fleshy, with dragging bosoms. The third is young and slender, not quite solid, whey-faced, with coils of pale green hair. Her filmy outline frames blurred trees. Wolves do not believe in wraiths or spirits, only the living and the dead, the eater and the eaten. Here are three voices made into visible beings. She gazes first at one and then the next. Fear ebbs away: curiosity has taken hold.

'Who are you?' she asks the old woman.

'I am Cailleach, and this is my sister Berthe —' she indicates the pale bloated creature with the pendulous breasts '— and that is Merrow, the youngest of the brood.' Merrow stares blankly. She is something like a jellyfish, suspended in salt water.

'Why are you here?' asks the wolf-child.

'We are always here.'

'I never saw you.'

'You never looked.'

This is true; they are not food. Which is a shame, as she is hungrier than ever. 'What do you want?'

Merrow smiles. 'It wastes no time,' she says.

'I'm not "it".'

'You ask who we are, but what do you call yourself?' asks pendulous Berthe. 'There are no others like you.'

'I'm Wolf!' she says.

Berthe touches her face with a moist finger. 'More like a human,' she says. 'Close to, you're nothing like a cub.'

'I'm born of wolves!'

'You may have suckled at their teats, but you're not their breed,' says Cailleach. 'But something other. Beneath that hair.'

'I never saw such an ugly creature,' says Merrow. 'So clawed and filthy.'

'You are young, and lack experience,' says Cailleach. 'There is nothing ugly in the world, only sights that we aren't used to. And almost anything is possible, in form, in family, in strange adaptation. Sometimes a creature brings up one who's not her own, if she is minded to. I knew a whale once, suckled an infant porpoise. She thrived and grew to a vast size.'

The three figures recede, like tide ebbing from the shingle, and questions linger in the air, foggy in the winter silence. There is no visible sign of movement, only a thrumming in the trees and a ripple around the edges of the clearing. Something changes, as night-dark fades before there's any sign of morning. Then, one by one, imperceptibly, they come back and stand near her.

Cailleach takes her hands and sets her upright. 'You

will come with us. We'll call you Wulva. We will teach you what we know. To begin, you must walk as we do.'

'But I belong here! And I can't walk that way. It hurts, and I need to smell the ground.'

'Do you want to starve? They've gone, the ones you've taken for your tribe. They won't be back; their bloodline's done.'

Cailleach takes something from her robe. A dead pigeon wrapped in oak-leaves. 'Eat this. And if you come with us, we can feed you with something better. Something from the pot.'

Wulva snatches the bird from Cailleach and tears the flesh with her teeth, spitting out the feathers. When she's finished, she wipes her mouth and nods to Cailleach, who takes her by the arm. The old creature's hand is long and claw-like, with yellow, twisted nails.

Deep into the darkening forest they go. Past wide trunks, under tangled branches. Wulva has never seen this part of the wood before, and she follows blindly, hungrily, knowing that she must trust the three who found her. Now the trees are closing in, forming a living cave. There is a stillness here, different from the rest of the forest. She sniffs and tries to understand what's new. A dun, dark quiet, a shaded listening; something watches from above. She looks up, but sees only reaching branches, creaking in the wind. All the trees here are yew, the undergrowth is thin and brown, each tree has its place, distinct and separate. The trunks are wider than any she has seen, wider than a standing wolf.

Cailleach leads the way. She comes to a tree far mightier than the others, twisted by some force of its own making, its branches reaching high above Wulva's head. There's an opening in the vast trunk, a crevice in the wood, and Cailleach climbs inside. The others follow, Wulva last of all. She sees a cavernous living place, a forest castle, which slowly creaks and shifts around them. Wulva runs her hands over the heart-wood; the sound of the outer forest fades.

The giant yew tree has many chambers, walkways, a host of secret and green-lit places. They contain strange objects, and Wulva marvels at them. Tables and chairs of carved oak and burnished elm, bedsheets and linens, goatskins and tapestries that smell of musk. It is a castle-sett, a palace-lair, a warren. At the very centre of the yew house, there is an opening — too small to call a clearing, more like the courtyard of a castle — and in the middle of that, a fire burns with a low flame but a great intensity. It has a strange scent, and Cailleach goes and tends to it, poking the logs and studying the shifting embers.

The sisters busy themselves, going hither and thither, bringing a wooden tub and various bottles and vials to the fire. Merrow brings armfuls of brightly coloured clothes, Berthe brings roots and a dead goat, while Cailleach gets a heavy book and consults it, running her fingers over the pages. Wulva, used to waiting, sits on her haunches, watching.

Cailleach looks up at her. 'This isn't our book,' she says. 'Books aren't our way. It's *theirs*.'

Wulva cocks her head. 'Theirs?'

'The mormaers. Back in their other times. Wizardry, monsters, killing.' Cailleach turns more pages. 'And what they call spells.'

'What is a mormaer?'

'Their word for leader,' says Cailleach. 'And as they do, so do the rest. Cutting and scything, burning and maiming. So that's how we name them. Another word is "human".' She looks at Wulva queerly. 'These are your people, though you were just a mewling bairn when you were lost.'

'But I don't know them. I don't see them.' Yet that is not quite true. Wulva has seen something of them. She knows Other Beast, the crashing hunter, breaking and tearing, his sudden shouts of laughter. In the river, casting his threads into the water. She has smelled his blood. And that flash he carries in his hand, the cut of silver, a long tooth for cutting throats.

Cailleach returns to her reading. 'This is what we must mend,' she says. She darts another glance at Wulva. 'They killed the wolves — *your* wolves. The one that suckled you, for what reason I can't tell. So the mormaers are your people, but your enemy too. Your blood is human, yet you milked a she-wolf's teat. That is a good place to begin.'

Before Wulva has time to ponder these strange words, Berthe and Merrow have seized hold of her, lifted her up and plunged her into the tub, which is now full of water. The fact that it is cold doesn't matter to Wulva, but what does alarm her is that they are using some queer-smelling stone, and scrubbing her with this. The dirt and filth of all her years of living are being scraped off, as is much of the fine hair that covers her arms and legs. She growls and flails, but it makes no difference. They take her out, wrap her in a rough cloth, and rub her dry. Blinking in the firelight, she is stunned into temporary quiet, and sits still as they cut her hair, watching the long locks falling to the ground around her. When they are done, it still falls well below her shoulders, and Merrow brushes it out, in long, firm sweeps, the bristles scraping her scalp. Something goes over her head, something smooth and sweet-smelling, and Merrow ties it up behind. Then Berthe gives her something cold and flat that glitters on one side. 'Look at yourself,' says Berthe. 'Who would have known that you were such a fine one, beneath the hair and mud?'

A creature is looking up from the glittering shape. It has wide, dark eyes and thick brows, pale skin, black hair like a raven's wing. 'What's this?' she says. She turns the mirror over. 'Where's it hiding?'

'It's you,' says Cailleach, screeching with laughter. 'You see? A mormaer. Now you must learn to act like them, since you are their lost daughter.'

'Me?' The face frowns at her. She has never seen anything like it. Bending closer, she goes eye-to-eye with it, so the cold obsidian touches her face, and then she knows. 'Me.'

Cailleach laughs again, and the sisters prepare food. Before she is allowed to eat, they bring a table and chairs, and show Wulva how to dine as they do, sitting upright with her hind legs hidden. She tears at the goat-meat with her nails and teeth, and Cailleach looks on calmly, and says to Berthe: 'She'll learn their manners later.'

V

It is a week after the Assumption of Mary: the day of their departure has arrived. As is the custom, the monks rise at dawn for Lauds, and proceed to the chapel in silence. Even in high summer, the early hours are cool, as the stone walls retain the memory of winter cold throughout the year. Rowan is kneeling with his eyes closed, chanting the familiar words, wondering when he will next do this in the company of the brethren. The chapel is filled with the monks' merging and flowing voices, and his spirit lifts in spite of himself as he joins the plainchant. The tenor is the foundation voice, and interwoven voices float above, as birds fly in the heavens. The plague has not destroyed them; the life of the abbey has prevailed, and will continue. His low mood is the result of thinking selfishly, as if the concerns of one man dominate the whole world. But the monastery is a place where many are made one, a microcosm of the Church itself. As one man, he is nothing, valuable only to Our Lord, who cares for every sinner, no matter how obscure. As part of this community, he has value, and a role to play. He thinks about the mission to the north. Surely he should rejoice in having work to do? That he is in the service of the priory, that the Reverend Father finds him useful? But he is not able to command any emotion beyond apprehension. He is only human, after all.

Brother Kenneth is sitting near the front of the chapel. He is always one of the first to arrive, and his voice is distinctive, rising above the collective plainsong. Rowan tries to organise his thoughts. One of the difficulties, in relation to the forthcoming journey, is that he can't imagine it, never having travelled north, and therefore he sees himself vanishing into a void. Kenneth will be familiar, only Kenneth. He swallows, and attempts to lose himself in prayer. But his mind won't be at peace. 'Leave your body at the door; here is the kingdom of souls, the flesh has nothing more to do with it.' So says Bernard of Clairvaux. And Rowan has taken heed of such exhortations. When he first came, he so craved wine that he hallucinated brimming jugs of burgundy when he was lying in the dormitory, and was so ill suited to the demands of worship that he chewed peppercorns during the office to stay awake. But that was many years ago, and the privations of the body are now part of his daily round. Returning to the outside world alarms him: while God protects, Lucifer is devious.

Rowan revels in the fervency of their devotion. Surely he can draw his strength from this, even when he has left the precincts of the abbey? Prayer is the answer; prayer and the example of the Saints. He must turn his eyes towards the Maker and away from sin. But oh dear. He has recalled another quotation — one of the perils of his calling as a scribe is that he might recall any number of wise sayings at any moment. 'Just as the oyster is safe within its shell, yet is prey to crabs and other enemies when it comes out, so the monk is safe within the convent walls, but outside is exposed to the snares of evil.' Rowan puzzles over this. He has never seen an oyster leave its shell, and wonders if it used to do so in the days in which they wrote the scriptures.

The prior sees them off, shielding his eyes from the bright sun as he looks up at them. Kenneth sits easily astride his mount, and his eyes wander from time to time to the road ahead, and the hills on the horizon. Rowan is already hot, and has not found a way to comfortably stow his pack. (He has kept this to a minimum, but certain items are essential: it contains his tunic, pumice stone, parchment roll, goose-quills, and a bundle of beeswax candles.) This is causing him additional anxiety. Furthermore, he is not confident about the stopper in his ink-horn, which he is carrying attached to a belt. What will happen if it leaks, and he has no ink to write with? Nothing seems fitting, or as it should be.

'Remember, this is important work you are about,' says Father Andrew. 'Our prayers go with you.'

'Thank you, Reverend Father. We shall do our best,' says Rowan.

'With luck, you will be there and back again by All Saints' Day.'

'I sincerely hope so! I had hoped we might be back before then. Before the weather turns.' Rowan tries — and fails — to keep a querulous note from his voice.

Kenneth shrugs, and turns Zeus's head. 'We can reach the North Road today if we make good time,' he says. 'Let's be on our way.'

Time is of great moment to Kenneth, who has a greater aptitude than Rowan for knowing the exact hour of day by instinct and the position of the sun. The prior has spoken of the king's acquisition of a mechanical clock, but Rowan has never seen such a thing, and the idea seems extraordinary. For him, time and the rituals of the monastery are inextricably connected, and during all his years there, he has had little need to judge the hour by the angle of the sun. Yet this is a skill that Kenneth uses with zeal: he can tell not just the hour but the minute, and it seems that their journey must proceed with military efficiency. Rowan's anxieties about being removed from the routines of the priory may be premature, for, as they ride, Kenneth informs him that they will be adhering strictly to the canonical hours during their mission.

'We shall be tested by this exposure to the world,' he says. 'What is womanish and unclean will present itself to us, no doubt, nature in its lowest form. But we are men of God, and of pure mind, so we shall repel what is earthbound, low, and bestial.'

'My thoughts entirely,' says Rowan, wiping the perspiration from his brow.

'We are divided from the order of communal life, but we have one another. We shall thus resist the numerous temptations of the Fiend.'

'You speak wisely, Brother Kenneth.'

But the prospect of their forthcoming Christian fortitude alarms him. Kenneth is bound to find him wanting.

'When we eat, we shall not listen to the gospels, as we do in the refectory, yet we can preserve the rule of silence and reflect on them. Of course, we shall wake nightly to say Matins, and rise at dawn for Lauds. We shall say brief prayers for the little offices before we break our fast at noon. We shall habitually have concluded the day's journey in time for Vespers. So the canonical hours fit naturally into a travelling day.'

'This all sounds very fitting. I am glad you have planned it all so clearly. I had assumed we would observe these prayer times, but, I confess, I hadn't thought about it with such precision.'

'Merely obedient, brother. And I am wont to be particular in matters of routine. It is part of my military training. For myself, I shall also take account of my spiritual welfare each morning, and draw up an agenda for the day, and in the evening I shall reflect on that.'

They proceed at a steady trot, following the track that

borders the river and heading east. Rowan's view is limited by the broad-brimmed hat he is wearing. From beneath it, he can see heath and dense woodland, the trees coming close to the south shore of the river. If he looks ahead, his view is of Kenneth and his mount, the latter now less skittish, as if the prospect of a journey is congenial to him. Hestia, on the other hand, seems indifferent to her surroundings, and moves with placid ease, as if being in a stable or the open air is all the same to her. He knows monks of a similar disposition, and in some ways they are blessed — it can be a great boon to pass through life in passive contentment. Did not Adam bite the apple because he wanted to know too much? Rowan is not made like the docile monks. In his former life in the scriptorium, he was cursed with curiosity. Is he still? Has he lost his desire for knowledge? He contemplates this as he passes through the tranquil countryside, beside the sparkling waters of the river. His illness has diminished his pleasures, Godly though they were, and sapped the energy on which he once depended. Turning in his saddle, he looks at the surrounding landscape, with its smooth and rounded slopes and the flat-topped mountains on the horizon. The sky is azure blue, the clouds flimsy and transparent. If this were a pilgrimage, he might find a little more purpose in the endeavour, might find more nourishment in it. When he was a boy, he longed to travel all the way to the Holy Land, to walk where Christ had walked, tread in his footsteps. But he was young then. Now he would rather leave such exploits to those who are more robust than he is.

A great stag is drinking from the river. It wades into the shallows, shaking droplets from its muzzle, scanning the riverbank as it splashes through the water. Mighty antlers tower above its head, its sturdy frame designed to bear the weight of them. An example, surely, of the Maker's attention to every detail, and His joy in His creation.

Without realising, Rowan has pulled on the reins and Hestia is slowing to a standstill. The stag drinks its fill and lumbers up onto the further shore. Kenneth is some way ahead. Rowan tries to kick the mare on, but she seems to have decided that they have reached a natural break in their journey. Pulling her head forward, she begins to graze on the vegetation that borders the pathway. Kenneth looks round and comes cantering back.

'What's the matter? Are you unwell?'

'No ... no more than usual. I was looking at a stag.'

'Brother Rowan, we don't have time to stand and stare at the world and all its marvels.'

'But the world is marvellous, is it not? And in looking at it and seeing it for the wonder that it is, are we not offering up our gratitude to God?'

'I dare say we are, but there are other matters in hand at the present moment.'

'That creature — the magnificence! The mystery of it!'

'Yes, stags are very wonderful, and roast venison makes an excellent dinner. Being admired for its beauty is not what nature is for. We must give thanks to God for it, as we must give thanks for all of Creation, and His Mercy. But while we are speaking, in this very moment, innumerable creatures are being eaten alive, or running for their lives, screaming with fear. This is all God's plan, the purpose of which has yet to be revealed.'

'Of course, you are right, but my spirits lifted at the sight of it.'

'Let us draw a line now. We must make good time. There is an inn some twenty miles ahead where I know we will pass a comfortable night, so I suggest that we attempt this. And furthermore, we must stick together. All kinds of undesirables plague these old ways. Now, take control of your mount and let's press on.'

They proceed, the bright sun illuminating the rolling landscape and the long curve of the river. Kenneth, up ahead, begins to sing the Sanctus, the words trailing behind him on the gentle summer wind:

Sanctus, Sanctus, Sanctus
Dominus Deus
Pleni sunt cæli et terra gloria tua.
Benedictus qui venit in nomine Domini.
Hosanna in excelsis.

It is shocking to hear the chant here, in the outside world, rather than enclosed in the stone-walled chapel, where the harmonies of the monks seem to possess some immortal potency. The sound seems fragile in comparison to the wild reaches of nature, stretching beyond his sight.

They are now entering an ancient woodland, the trees gradually closing above them. On the path ahead, sunbeams dapple the ground, showing here a clump of yellow globeflowers and there the bulbous outline of a death-cap mushroom. Rowan slows down once again, mesmerised by the singing and the scene. He is transported to his childhood: memories surface that have been buried, by worship, by discipline, more lately by tiredness and grief. He sees a small boy running through the bracken, beating his way along with a stick, utterly lost in his own world. He senses, for an instant, the forest as this child does, filled with scents and shadows.

Sanctus, Sanctus, Sanctus

When they emerge from the woodland, an hour or so later, he sees that clouds have gathered overhead, and the day is colder. The track still follows the river valley, and the valley sides swoop upwards towards the rounded hills. Rowan realises how stiff and uncomfortable he feels, and how sore his hips are. He reins in Hestia and slithers down to the ground, relieved to be out of the saddle. Taking hold of the mare's bridle, he leads her on.

Kenneth looks back over his shoulder. 'What on earth are you doing now?'

'My hips are hurting.'

'Then offer up the pain to God. We'll be halfway to nowhere at nightfall if we proceed at your shambling pace.'

'Then let it be so. I can't do otherwise.'

Kenneth wheels his horse round and comes trotting back. 'Look, brother. This really will not do. The rider must take command of the beast. They like it when they know who's in charge. It calms them. I'm beginning to wonder if you are fitted for this journey.'

'I asked the Reverend Father exactly the same thing.'

'Well, I bow to his superior judgement, but it seems to me that a sturdier fellow than yourself would have been preferable. Surely someone else could make a copy, or whatever it is you'll be about.'

'Father Andrew thought not. It is not a question merely of copying, but of finding the right document in the first place, and of extracting, from that, exactly the information needed.'

Kenneth has already tired of the subject. 'That may be so. But at this point the skills of *manliness* are required, rather than *scholarship*, so my advice is to make more effort. The more you ride, the sooner you will become accustomed to the exercise.'

'I have had my fill for today. There is only so much I can do, no matter what you say. No doubt we will proceed more quickly later on.'

'God's teeth!' cries Kenneth. He turns round and

canters ahead, leaving Rowan to the contemplation of the empty countryside and his companion's unexpected use of strong language. He hopes this will be included in Kenneth's reflections on his Christian piety at the close of day.

The sky is darkening, and there's a dank chill in the air — rain is on the way. He watches Kenneth vanishing into the distance. A man is always in God's hands; it is just more apparent when abroad in the outside world like this, rather than working in the abbey garden, pulling weeds. Walking side by side with his horse, he senses a mutual understanding between them. She seems to like the slow pace, and nuzzles his shoulder, as if to reassure him. The first drops of rain fall, lightly to begin with, and then in a soft, relentless deluge, soaking his habit and gently blinding him. He can hear only the gushing river and the squelching of his feet in the mud, and fears that his progress is even slower. What time is it? Late afternoon, surely; hunger gnaws his belly, but he is used to that. The grey skies darken; he shivers. Rowan plods on, noting the poor state of his sandaled feet, scotched with mud. The rain is so heavy that it casts a pall over the scene, so that he might be walking inside a cloud. Looking up, he sees that he's on the brow of a hill. The road stretches ahead of him, following the curve of the land. He has a sudden feeling of immense and tearful happiness, as if he never saw the world before.

VI

The yew house seems not to end, nor to stay as it is from one day to the next. As a tree shifts and trembles in the wind, as it sheds its leaves and puts on new ones, so the yew house changes not only with the seasons, but with the hours of the day. It is home to owls and egrets, voles and wood mice; it hosts sprouting pustules of fungi, mushrooms as big as a man's head, tiny spoors like the eyes of ants. The doors to its rooms open and then disappear, and the rooms themselves are not of regular size, nor do they remain the same shape. The house breathes and watches; its corridors are soft and permeable, its ceilings sometimes open to clear sky. The three sisters live sometimes apart, sometimes together. Wulva is never sure when she will find them. At night, the house is crowned with dark sky, the moon casts silver shadows across the fire clearing, the fire itself burns blue and violet, and the old crone Cailleach sits beside it, deep in thought.

That's her domain; it is Cailleach who remembers. The past is trapped inside her mind, twisting invisibly, and sometimes she will talk about it. After sundown, she will tell her stories. Stillness and quietness follow Cailleach, but when she says something must be done, it is done. Berthe is busy, always making, fetching, carrying. It is Berthe who prepares the food each night, who traps the beasts and kills them, who gathers wild herbs and forages for roots. Her wide, clumsy body seems never to stop moving. When they have eaten, she works on a great tapestry of silk and spider web. Merrow rarely speaks and seems caught up in a spell of her own making, watching herself in the looking glass, combing her hair and singing strange songs of mermaids, whale roads, drowned gods, and underwater queens. The three move and glide about the yew house, bringing flotsam treasures, furnishing its chambers with the lost possessions of the mormaers, as well as the queer objects that the forest sheds and births.

Wulva is not aware of learning, or changing, or that time is passing. Each day seems like the others, patterned by weather and seasons, illuminated greenly, shadowed in earthly mystery. Yet one day, she finds that she is walking on her hind legs in a silk dress, and has no desire to reach down to the ground again, nor to grunt nor growl, and her language is that of the sisters. The wolf-tongue is still familiar, and her thoughts are still formed of pictures she learned to make when she was with her wolf-mother: pictures of light, of dark, of sound, of smell. But gradually, since the sisters took her in, she has learned to speak with them, in what she supposes is their language. Over time, she learns another lesson: that this tongue the sisters teach her is also that of Other Beast. This language comes to form her conscious mind, though her dreaming is another matter.

Now, when Other Beast comes crashing by, she can catch odd words and phrases, though she does not know what they mean. She does know that Other Beast is wasteful, leaving much dead meat behind. The sisters feast on their carrion: roe deer, foxes, boar. Wulva eats with a knife, from a silver platter, and she has her own chamber, high above the green, a rocking eyrie furnished with a wooden bedstead and a tapestry of the wild hunt.

A year passes, and then another. Wulva grows taller, and her mind seeks to know more. Her face is thinner, longer, trapped in the obsidian mirror. Merrow rubs herbal potions into her skin, and combs her hair with oils and perfumes. All the time, she feels the sisters watching her.

'I am "mormaer", but not,' she says one day to Cailleach, picking her words with care.

'That's right. Lost in the great forest.'

'And only "wolf" by nurture.'

'Yes.'

'How do you know that?' asks Wulva. She sees translucent sea-green Merrow loitering close by.

'Because of what I've seen in my long life,' says Cailleach.

Wulva considers this. 'There may yet be things beyond your knowledge.'

'No one can know everything. Apart from the mormaers' all-seeing God. You will discover more about this later.'

'So what are you, and Berthe, and Merrow?'

'Ha!' says the maiden Merrow, and her skirts flick like a fish-tail.

Wulva has Cailleach's full attention now. 'There are different mormaer names for us, but none of them fit entirely.'

'Such as what?'

'Some call us Norns, or Furies. Some think we're their own kind, only mad or wicked and in need of punishment. They talk of witchcraft. But we are more than that, and less, and slippery. They think they see us; they think their senses form the world. And they are wrong. We are numerous and multiple, we are shifting and permeable. Our skin shrinks and stretches. We're porous, boneless, edgeless, seeping into myths and dreams and histories. We are small enough to crawl in the long grass, and pass unseen; we might drown in a drop of dew, and yet survive for centuries. No man knows our lifespan. They can't explain us, name us as they may. Their understanding is that of a mouse inside its hole, who sees a universe in a heap of straw. Mormaers' words are house-planks, flat and crude.'

'You are not "wolf", not "mormaer", but other?'

Cailleach nods.

'And what do you call yourselves?'

'We don't need to name ourselves. We're sisters.'
'Although you are so different from each other?'
'We live with what is given. And names are shifty.'
'But when you found me ... what did you think I was?'
'Ha!' says Merrow, again. Then she fades away, leaving a shadow of deep green.

The longer she lives with the sisters, the more the yew house says to her. It is not one house, not one place, because living trees have made it, unfelled, undamaged, bending their branches to make rounded, green-lit chambers. The stories she hears aren't formed from words; the leaves stir and breathe, and she remembers. In the dark sky there are a thousand thousand points of feeling; the star-thick universe is full of stories, and below, the root-mind, brindling and twisting among worm-ends, old shapes gently vanishing, new roots sapped from death.

The yew house thrums with life, and even in the cold of winter there is the liquid song of blackbirds, the guttural croaks of crows, the night cries of hares and stags. Its walls whisper, the wind rattles its branches, the undergrowth is busy with voles and badgers. The roots of the yew trees suck in the deep scent of the soil, and their topmost branches catch the moonlight, the dense breeze, the lightness of the sun. Wulva can climb the trees even in her fine gowns, and she pays no attention to the rips and tatters, which are always mended when she wakes the next day. She watches the sisters going out into the forest, about their business, scavenging, collecting, killing. These deaths are usually for the pot. Rabbits and pigeons, for the most part, sometimes a wild goat. Cailleach kills with her long claw-nails. Berthe uses the art of strangulation. Merrow suffocates her prey.

But it is not only creatures for the pot that they bring home with them. There are books and scrolls as well, and Cailleach keeps guard over these, stored in an oak casket that is bound with iron bands.

'I have taught myself the skill of reading the mormaers' words,' she says to Wulva. 'There is one tongue that they call "Latin" and another they call "Scots". Now I will pass this on to you. But you will have to work hard.'

Wulva picks up a book and smells it. She likes the scent — heavy, rich, exotic. Without opening the covers, she senses the shape of unknown lands.

'You will read them all before you leave us,' says Cailleach.

Wulva looks at her. 'Where shall I go?'

'You will find out when you are ready.'

These are human words, written on goatskin parchment with ink of oak-gall. The words are in Latin, which Cailleach translates to Gaelic. They sit with an open book between them, reading the histories of Pliny and puzzling out the tales of Ovid. Words and pictures form and dance in Wulva's mind. Acmon, who turned into a bird; Actaeon, who became a stag; Byblis, who transformed into a nymph. The pictures in her head merge with the things that she remembers, and the woven figures on the tapestry that is hanging in her chamber. She sees the wolves running with fauns and dryads, Other Beast on horseback, chasing Charybdis, who becomes a sea-monster.

It takes many months of puzzling and frustration, of working out and memorising marks on parchment, but she learns to read the books herself. Each one takes her to a place unknown and terrible, to wars and journeys, to the edge of blackest water, to the deaths of children. This is the mormaer-law; this is the language that they speak. Cailleach shows her their great book Bible, and she reads this through and through, and marks the opening, as Cailleach says she must.

'Mark the opening,' says Cailleach.

'I have.'

'Read it out loud to me.'

Wulva reads:

'So God created man in His own image, in the image of God created He him; male and female created He them. And God blessed them, and God said unto them, Be fruitful, and multiply, and replenish the earth, and subdue it: and have dominion over the fish of the sea, and over the fowl of the air, and over every living thing that moveth upon the earth.'

This is the strongest mormaer-spell, says Cailleach, and by this they live.

VII

Walking with Hestia gives Rowan a new perspective on the landscape. He does not have the height that he would have in the saddle, so there is less of a view. But the companionship he shares with the beast as they amble along, hour after hour, gives an insight of a different kind, of what might be termed the equine position. Hestia's interests are chiefly focused on various types of grass and vegetation, and he is obliged to be quite firm about this. Left to her own devices, she would simply graze and travel perhaps half a league. So he keeps her on a slack rein, and Hestia nibbles what she fancies as she moves along. So contented is she with this arrangement that from time to time she nuzzles him gently, as if to express her pleasure and affection.

At first Rowan sings various hymns, then songs he remembers from his boyhood. But after a while, he lapses into silence, and listens to the sound of Hestia, interminably munching, trying to sense her ruminant thoughts. What does a horse think about? Fields, sweet hay, the touch of its companions? And of man, its master? A horse might have a poor opinion of a man, seeing all the worst things in him. It is ridden by man, which can't be pleasant. Does it have memory? Does it speculate? Make calculations? He presumes not. There is more likelihood of introspection in a dog or pig. Hestia's mind, lacking human language, might focus on various subjects in a blurred and vegetarian way. But perhaps there are areas in which she improves upon the human in her thinking; areas, for example, that are tedious, drawn out, mired in repetition. Here, she may have slow, inchoate modes of understanding inaccessible to man.

Such thoughts are almost certainly blasphemous, and he would never voice them. In any case, a feeling of deep calm comes over him, like that Lenten sense of complete immersion in some other way of being, but without the rumbling stomach. It is diverting but exhausting to be thus engaged. By early evening, he is dizzy with tiredness, and barely registers the fact that Kenneth is waiting for him by the pathway, an expression of peevish impatience on his face. When they see a watermill in the distance, Rowan cries out happily: 'Praise God! Praise Him for His succour.'

But Kenneth says nothing, only narrows his eyes and flicks a fly off Zeus's mane.

Eventually, they come to a standstill by the mill. It is a mean little building no bigger than a crofter's cottage, and having an appearance both makeshift and neglected, with curved walls and a sagging roof, half submerged by thistles and hogweed. It's more like a bird's nest than a proper human habitation. The mill-wheel revolves steadily, churning the crashing water. Rowan is stirred by this familiar sound, the rhythmic creak and splash. It reminds him of his boyhood. Every river in the land has its busy mill-wheels, just as every home has bread upon the table. There is no reply when they knock, but when they raise the latch, the door swings open.

'I regard this as an invitation. A mill like this, on the way to the North Road, they must be accustomed to all manner of travellers passing the night,' says Kenneth. 'And there must be someone near at hand. The mill can't function unattended.'

Rowan longs to rest, to go inside, to eat and drink, and, finally, to sleep. But he is hesitant. 'It seems a little presumptuous, to enter when there is no one in. Should we wait awhile?'

'You may do so if you wish. I am going to put the horses in the stable and then refresh myself. A soldier does not turn down a chance like this.'

Rowan enters the cottage, too tired to argue any further. It is simply furnished with a wooden table and two benches, with a ladder at the rear leading, he supposes, to a bed chamber. It is clean, however, and there is a cooking pot sitting on the hearth, giving out a most delicious smell. By the fireside is an elderly mouser, with flecked green eyes and queerly mangled ears set close to its head. After staring at Rowan for a moment, the cat shuts its eyes with an air of indifference. Feeling somehow reassured, Rowan sits down at the table. There is a loaf of bread, a jug of ale, and two cups. Should he take a drink? The cat opens its eyes and stares again, and there is something in this gaze that stops him. Rowan takes his drinking horn from his satchel and drinks from that instead. Not much of the small-beer he was given that morning remains, but there is enough to last until morning if he is careful.

When Kenneth comes in from the stable, Rowan notices that his face is flushed from the sun. 'I am hungry!' he announces. 'What's cooking in the pot?'

'Shouldn't we wait until our host returns?'

'If they were here, then they would tell us to eat our fill.'

'Yes, but ...' Rowan shifts uncomfortably in his seat, unsure how to express his doubt. Not only does it seem rude to eat without the cottager, something else is stopping him. 'There is a certain ... I don't feel ...'

'What, brother? There's food, the door is unlocked, and we are ravenous. The Lord has provided for us; He is guarding us on our journey. Let us give thanks for His all-seeing love, rather than question His bounty.'

'In the old tales ...' Rowan breaks off, unable to voice his foolish thoughts.

'What?'

'There is much wisdom in ancient legend ...'

'Brother, you are tired and wandering in your thoughts. I dare say there is much to recommend the ancient legends, though I fail to see how that relates to this present circumstance. They are mere fancies, and we live by the word of our One God.'

'Yet there are little shards of wisdom there, of warning. You may think me fanciful, but I was thinking of Persephone, who ate the pomegranate seeds and was obliged to stay in the Underworld for half the year.'

Kenneth shrugs. 'I don't look to pagan tales for guidance.'

Rowan tries to put it another way, but fails. The mill is warm and comfortable, and yet he can't dispel this feeling of unease.

'Come now, Rowan! Let us say our prayers, then no ill will befall us.'

They bow their heads and intone: *Benedic, Domine, nos et haec tua dona quae de tua largitate sumus sumpturi, per Christum Dominum nostrum. Amen.*

Kenneth swigs back a cup of ale, then wipes his lips. 'A word of advice to you, Brother Rowan. When food presents itself, it must be eaten. We've done a good few miles despite your best endeavours to proceed at a slug's pace. Tomorrow we shall go further, God willing. So eat up, and fortify yourself.'

But Rowan can't bring himself to do the same. He takes another sip from his drinking horn. 'I shall fill this from the river in the morning,' he says. 'Though I am not sure of its quality.' One of the monastery amenities he took for granted was the well, and the unending supply of cold, clean water.

'You'll not risk drinking a fine draught of ale from this flagon, but you will drink water mired with cow-dung and the like? Good luck to you.' Kenneth goes over to the fireside and helps himself to stew. When he lifts the lid, there is an aroma of mutton and rosemary. Rowan's mouth begins to water. But he merely unwraps what remains of his bread and cheese and eats it glumly. The bread is dry, and the cheese has sweated in the summer heat.

'You are a strange fellow,' says Kenneth, refilling his cup. 'Surely you know, as we all do who are civilised men, that there is only one religion? One God, one Heaven, one Way? Yet you are behaving as if the old beliefs still guide you. Come, you are only here because you are a scholar, an educated man! I advise you to behave like one, for your own good if not for mine.'

Rowan refolds the cloth that wrapped his bread. He is tired and still hungry, and has no will to engage in argument. For a while there is silence. Kenneth finishes his stew and sits back in his seat, at his leisure. 'Whatever your intellectual gifts, I doubt you will last as far as Edinburgh, particularly if you decide to starve yourself. You are already skin and bone.'

'I was always thin, even in boyhood. And since the plague, my appetite has diminished.'

'Even after a day on horseback? You'll have to mend your ways or take the consequences.' Kenneth tilts his seat back. 'For myself, I'm glad to be on the open road. I had forgotten how it feels, not knowing where you will spend the night, riding towards a new horizon every morning.

It reminds me of my time in Spain, fighting the Infidel at Algezir and Granada.'

'Your present life must seem very quiet and uneventful after such adventures. What terrifying times those must have been!'

'The Infidel is not like the Christian. He slaughters for his pleasure. But God gave me strength.'

'And — you were fighting for a Scottish knight?' Rowan knows little about the Crusades.

Kenneth looks away. 'As it happens, I was in the service of an English knight.'

'Oh. That must have been somewhat uncomfortable, given their ways.'

'The modern soldier takes up service where he can. I wished to fight the Infidel, and taking up arms for this fellow gave me the chance to do so.'

They are silent for a moment, Rowan feeling, as he so often does, that he knows little of the world.

'Some people use the word "mercenary", though that term is ugly and misleading,' says Kenneth, gruffly. 'My life is given up to the service of the Maker, no matter what the business I am about. His Love protects us, His Wisdom guides us.' Kenneth drains his cup. 'But yes, the priory is quiet, that is true. Yet I take great comfort in its order, make no mistake. There is balm in the ecclesiastic calendar. That is my lodestone, the orderer of my days, just as once they were surrendered to armed service.'

Rowan tries to organise his thoughts, and fails. He sees images from the plague time, and all is chaos and confusion. The sick room, where he was summoned after the infirmarian died, and where he was obliged to take his place as best he could. The old prior Father Paul thought Rowan's skill in growing herbs must now be used to aid the sick and dying. His commands were, as usual, imperious. And then Father Paul himself was dead, his face black with pestilence. Just like any other man. Where was God then? The question was often asked by those in their last hours, but the living carried on, praising God as they had always done. He understands this well; the rigours of daily worship have also supported him. Yet what torment! Time reeled, from dizzying, confounding speed to slow, agonising watching. How long, how long, a quick death takes! How terrible the death throes of a hale young man! He sees now the blurring, shifting, and eventual dark that overtook him when it was his turn to succumb. As he slipped into a pain-drenched semi-consciousness, a heating madness, he felt something unexpected. Relief. He no longer had to minister to these poor souls he could not help. He would lie peacefully in the grave and be forgotten. He might have hoped for visions of the Hereafter, the certainty of Divine Love, but these were not forthcoming. All he could envisage was the lasting peace of earthly burial. The prospect did not appal him. But then the Lord God intervened and saved him. He recalls now, with a jolt of horror, his return. Pain came first. No words, no knowledge of who he was, or what had taken place. His surroundings followed, in dim perspectives, unknown, in no way explicable. The ceiling of the infirmary, ridges of plaster, the dark rafters that seemed like bars above his head. He thought the cracks in the plaster might be the sides of a whale, at one point, a silvered water-beast. Then he thought it might be a map of unknown oceans. When he then came to some semblance of awareness, he thought that he might be in purgatory, not knowing how that would look, and after that, he wondered if he was enduring some sort of temporal imprisonment. He certainly felt that he had sinned or committed a crime. After that, things began to name themselves. The flickering glow was *candlelight*, the soft aroma *lavender*. He wept then. When he realised it was the monastery sick room. He had so wanted to be somewhere else, transformed, to look down or backward and be done.

He comes to, realising that Kenneth is staring at him, bemused.

'Forgive me, my mind wandered for a moment.'

'God moves in mysterious ways,' says Kenneth. 'Casting us together on this adventure. There could not be two brothers in the abbey less alike than we two.'

'It's true. A quiet life always suited me.'

Kenneth stretches and yawns. 'I've seen the world, let's just say that. A man like you would not want to hear about it. The monk's life? Well, I offer it up to God, and I know that our prayers keep other men from hellfire. But it's the open road where I'm happiest, I must confess. Even on such a fool's errand as this one, dispatched to do some clerking with a half-baked weakling who can't even ride a horse.'

Could Kenneth be drunk after two cups of ale? Rowan has never heard him so voluble, nor cruel. 'You are tired, brother, and so am I. I shall retire to bed,' he says stiffly. 'The morning may improve my spirits and your manners.'

'You forget — it is time for Vespers,' says Kenneth.

They repeat the prayers together, and Rowan strains to feel good Christian love for Kenneth. When they have finished, he takes a rush-light up to the loft, where he finds a straw mattress and some blankets. Lying down, he attempts to pray, but the words seem frail and far off. He tries to sleep. His mind runs back to the plague time: again and again he sees Father Paul's dead face, the visions of the infirmary he took for purgatory. He survived the plague, and no one else did. Those ruddy boys, the older brothers, steeped in pious learning. Once afflicted, off they went, one by one. For the first time, he wonders if that marked him out for some particular calling. Foolish weakling, is he? That is yet to be confirmed.

After a while, he hears Kenneth ascend the ladder and lie down beside him. Before long, he is snoring lavishly, more hog than man. When the rush-light burns out, Rowan listens to the night sounds: an owl hooting, a fox barking, the rhythmic splashing of the mill-wheel.

VIII

Nature is the habitation of the sisters, but for Wulva there are other plans, beyond nature, outside the forest, where the land has been cleared so that the sky is ripped open, and there Wulva knows she must go, one day.

Under Cailleach's tutelage, Wulva learns to measure time by observing the movement of the sun and moon and planets, and by the operation of an hourglass and its falling sand. There is time in each day, not just the length of doing a thing — time that can be marked and measured as it passes. And there is larger time, a dwelling-place, of days and weeks and months, each held within the other. Larger again are years, winter to winter, divided by midsummer. The time she has been with the sisters is three years, and her height has been chiselled into the side of a towering yew tree. She is now five inches taller than when she came. She has almost forgotten that she walked on four legs, and that her skin was covered in soft down; almost forgotten the pleasure of eating a kill when it's still warm. Now she is something new. Merrow brushes out her hair, deep glossy brown. In the evening, by the fire in the centre of the clearing, Berthe whispers in her ear. Sometimes, Berthe scatters seeds into the fire, and the flames burn blue and green and purple. Then Wulva sees what has been and what is yet to come. But she can make no sense of these visions. She roams through the forest, as she once did with the wolves, learning new secrets, hidden in its twisting vastness. And she helps the sisters with their daily tasks, foraging for vetches and acorns, and looking after their hens and pigs. Her favourite pig, saved from the pot, is Iochtar.

The sisters are the queens of night-fear. Dark shadows flicker in the trees, but they don't heed them. They are not afraid of ogres, or hobgoblins, or banshees, or kelpies, or bean-nighes, or the horse-faced nuckelavee, most dreadful of them all. No. There is no growling, creeping, tumescent bodach, no grasping, starving phantom, no long-toothed prowler or foul-breathed demon of the Underworld that can scare them. Wulva knows them. The trembling, crumbling, rotting ground, which consumes and brings forth, which makes corpses into flowers, can do them no ill. It may eat and seep and swallow as it likes. They will walk in the shadows, sit mute upon fresh graves, listen to the death-cries of the night's prey, and it's all one, the depthless hunger of the Earth, that ceaseless mongrel pageant of death and fornication.

There are many ways of learning, as seeds are carried in the wind, on the beaks of flying birds, or trodden and transported by wild creatures. Wulva has learned the forest from the wolves; she knows their scent, their stealth. Now Cailleach teaches her to see through other eyes. Less than wolves, smaller, weaker, those who know their flesh is meat. They are swivel-eyed, taut-necked, alive to the threat of tooth and claw. A spider spins its thread from rowan leaf to oak branch, the sun dries rain on glittering grasses, and dusk fills shade with coming night. Badger-shaped, she hunts and forages, snout to the mossy ground, digging and slashing with her forepaws, feasting on slippy, loamy worms, lapping from night-scented streams, dreaming of wolf-jaws and waking with a twitch.

Sometimes Wulva soars with eagle-wings, as high as drifting cloud. Below spin mountains, greenwood, heathland, white cliffs, surging gannets. Smaller birds wheel below her; waves break and foam against black rocks. When she flies lower, her sight pierces the waves, fixing on gleans of herring, silver-backed and silent. Then she bulks and swells into a whale, surging on one breath under riptides; dark water booms, cool green fathoms repeat her song, she dines on rippling krill.

The days are vivid, charged with life and purpose. At night, she lies in her tree-top chamber and the wind shakes it gently. She hears the wolf-song, the demon howl, the call that makes the black night colder. Once, she meets a grizzled she-wolf in a clearing. But its yellow eyes are blank, and they are strangers to each other. Restless, she listens to the sound of what is yet to come.

It is spring; the forest is singing and awakening all around her. Bright leaves make patterns against the sky. They leave the yew house and set out into the forest. The air is bright, and there is dew on the ground. The piglet Iochtar follows them. They walk quickly, pushing through new undergrowth, passing pools and grottoes, grazing roe deer and rooting hogs. Cuckoos call from the trees above, and there are the cries of woodpigeons. Yet Wulva feels a growing sense of unease: this is not a path she knows. Cailleach forges through the greenwood, parting the foliage with her long fingers. From time to time, she looks behind to see if Wulva is following, but she does not acknowledge her presence in any other way. Meanwhile, Iochtar is in a frenzy of happiness, zigzagging this way and that way across their path, grunting quietly to himself at each new smell.

At last, they come to the edge of the forest. There is a long, stony road ahead of them. There is no sign of human habitation, and there's a curious silence. Cailleach stops and looks around her.

'Yes,' she says. 'This is the place. I shall come no further. They know me round here, and that does not suit our purpose.'

'What place do you mean? I see nothing here!'

'They call it Alba. All you need to do is follow this road.' Cailleach points south. 'Keep to the track, and you will find them.'

'But *who*?'

'They are called Macduff. They will protect you, and treat you as their own. We took you in because we needed someone to live among the mormaers. Which your appearance is well fitted for, and you have learned your lessons well.'

'My appearance? What do you mean?'

'This is your hour, your moment,' says Cailleach. 'I will not say any more. Anything else you need to know will be revealed to you in time, and until then, your ignorance will be an aid to your deception. See this old oak?' She points to a blasted, twisted tree. 'I will meet you here, exactly one year from today, and you must tell me what you have seen and heard. And each year after that, we shall do the same. Do you follow me? Mark the date well — it's Alban Eiler, when night and day are equal, and summer is on its way. Serve us faithfully, and you will not regret it. Also, make them a present of the pig.'

'But *why* am I going there?' cries Wulva, afraid. 'What am I meant to *do*? I don't understand!'

Cailleach says nothing, only turns and disappears into the forest.

For a moment, Wulva stands motionless, aghast. The breath has gone out of her. But Iochtar runs around, busy and cheerful, and she is glad of his company. She looks at the path that Cailleach showed her, and sniffs the air, as she used to. The stillness and silence perplex her. She looks back at the forest, and the glowering trees. There, the darkness beckons. All that she has ever known lies in that wood. Its strangeness is her strangeness, and she doesn't fear it. Ahead, there is the bleak curve of the road, and beyond that an outline of distant peaks, misted by dank cloud. From somewhere, far off, she hears a sound at last, a blur of noise. Straining to hear more plainly, she sets off along the path.

After walking for an hour or more, she sees a blunt shape on a hilltop. She knows it from the books that she has read. *Castle*, she thinks. *Mormaers*. As she approaches, it grows in size, and she can make out smaller buildings around its edges, like puppies suckling their tired mother. Iochtar runs ahead, snuffling in the undergrowth. He has no fear of mormaers, or unknown castles, nor any thought for the future. Yet Wulva thinks of what she knows of Other Beast, who came into the forest and killed the wolves. Fear is what keeps most creatures alive, supposing they are fast enough, and lucky. For a moment, she wonders if she and her pig might turn and run, leaving both forest and castle behind them. But the land around is boggy and barren, marked here and there with tree stumps. Where would they go? So she carries on, and the castle grows yet larger, and the noises within its walls yet louder, and before long, she is crossing the drawbridge, with Iochtar trotting after her.

IX

When the monks come down next morning, there is no sign of the decrepit cat, but an old woman is sitting by the fire. She might be as old as the house itself, from the look of her; she has the same air of vegetable antiquity, with a pocked and lumpen face resembling a turnip. Her forehead lowers over her eyes like a rocky outcrop, her skull is almost hairless — she has no hood or wimple. Rowan wonders if she is in full possession of her wits. But her green eyes, when she turns to look at them, are clear and watchful.

'God you keep,' she says, seeming unsurprised to see them. 'I hope you passed a comfortable night?'

'I fear we have imposed on your hospitality,' says Rowan. 'We were tired and hungry after a long day's travel and we —'

'This is as good a place for travellers to rest as any,' she says, in a rasping, mannish voice.

'Quite satisfactory,' says Kenneth, with the air of a man impatient to be off.

Rowan takes out his scrip. 'Let us pay you — what is your price for meal and board?' he asks.

But the old woman waves him away.

'Then with our thanks we shall depart forthwith,' says Kenneth. 'We must reach our next port of call by sundown, and there is no time to lose.'

'There, you see, is the way that you may repay me. In kind,' she says.

'I am afraid I don't follow you,' says Kenneth.

'These days, I am too old to walk far, and it's a long time since I owned a mule — oh, long before either of you were even thought of. I would beg a ride.'

'That is quite impossible ...' says Kenneth, while Rowan at the same instant cries: 'Of course ...'

'Where are you going?' asks Rowan.

'Death is my destination,' she says. 'And also yours, unless you are Almighty God Himself.'

'I am resigned to my mortality in this form, though I look forward to the day that I am joined for Eternity with my Maker, along with all who repent truly of their sin,' says Kenneth.

'In the more immediate future, we are bound for the North Road, God willing, and you are welcome to come with us,' says Rowan.

'God bless you, young man.'

Rowan feels that he has already received his earthly reward for this small kindness: no one has called him 'young' for years.

Kenneth gives Rowan a dark look. 'How will we make

good time if we are carrying a passenger? We must make haste; we cannot dawdle as we did yesterday.'

'She shall ride pillion,' says Rowan. 'If you are willing, madam? To ride behind me?'

'Madam, indeed,' mutters Kenneth under his breath, as if he has forgotten that respect is owed to the aged, even if they are humble and obscure. But that is how they proceed. The day is sunny and cloudless, and the air swarms with buzzing insects. For a while, they ride along, listening to the bleating of sheep and the river's gushing song. Kenneth looks pale and sweaty, and occasionally swats at midges.

The old woman clings tight to Rowan, as light and skinny as a child. Her touch gives him a strange sensation. He looks at the passing landscape, the gentle slope of the surrounding forest, the crags that break the treeline here and there, the kites that circle slowly high above, sensing a world beneath what is visible. And his hearing, normally so blunted, seems to pick up the sounds of wood-mice, crickets, voles. He feels, for a full ten minutes, that he is a fox running through bracken, a long green tunnel with the smell of fresh blood at its end.

The hills are flattening slightly, and the trees form strange, lopsided shapes: they are approaching the coast. Seabirds swoop and call above their heads, and the wind is brisk and chilly. Rowan scans the horizon, wondering if the sea is visible yet, but can see only the clean sweep of the sky. 'The sea' is a sharp picture in his head, from the time before he came into the monastery. He recalls two trees with narrow trunks and leaves of bright spring green. The road ends between them, so they form a sort of gateway to a wide, pale beach. Beyond that, there is a line of dark blue and a wide and cloudless sky. He has no recollection of going nearer, diving into the water, or feeling the sand beneath his feet. And yet those trees and the dark blue line bring him such joy that it might be a holy vision. Not that he, humble as he is, has ever had such a vision, only the imagined picture of how such a thing might be.

At length, he makes out a dark line on the distant horizon and feels a jolt of joy and wonder.

'Can it be? After all these years, just as it was. A domain between the dry land and the sky?'

'It can indeed,' says the old woman.

And he does not question, until later, how this conversation came to be.

The road now leads into a gentle valley; the river winds among the pinewoods, ending in a wide estuary, banked with yellow sand. Here the wind is stronger, pulling at his cloak and ruffling Hestia's mane. At the edge of the estuary, he can see the walls of a town.

'There's an inn, close to the gates,' says the old woman. 'You'll get a clean bed and a decent supper for a good price.'

'Where shall we take you?' asks Rowan.

'I'm coming to the inn with you. They won't charge you much extra.'

'Curse the woman,' says Kenneth. But he does not attempt to argue.

The other guests are mostly common fellows, dicing and playing cross and pile on the taproom floor. Two more refined-looking gentlemen are engrossed in a chess game. After supper, the old woman sits on the settle, her bare, misshapen feet close to the fire. Then she sleeps, muttering unintelligibly. At nightfall, she wakes with a start. 'I've come a long way, quite a distance further than I intended,' she says, addressing the room at large. 'And if you care to listen, I'll tell you a tale the like of which you never heard before.'

'There will be no need for that,' says Kenneth.

But a small group assembles around the fireside. There are expectant looks, and the old woman warms her hands, biding her time.

'The tale I have to tell is not a pretty one,' she says eventually. 'It will make you long for daybreak. But I hope that you will hear me.'

'We like the one about Grendel,' cries a pot boy, cheekily. 'Do you know it?'

Someone shushes him.

'I know the *tales* of Grendel,' she says. 'There are many. And those of spectres and hell-wains, dragons and sea-worms, damsels and knights holy and depraved. All the tales that you have heard, and more besides. But I speak only of what I've seen with my own eyes.'

Her gaze returns to the shifting pile of logs. The listeners at the fire are silent, waiting.

'We are all agog, I can assure you,' says the inn-keeper. 'I'll fetch you a cup of cider.'

'I'd like a bit of cake as well.'

He disappears, and the old woman pulls her cloak more tightly around her.

Rowan shivers, though the summer night isn't cold, and thinks of the world beyond the fire-lit circle. Tales from his childhood gather, looming like banked cloud. He thinks of forests, mountains, lochs, troll-caves, banshees, weird creatures moving noiseless among broken rocks. He recalls the words his mother used to say at his bedside, once the more conventional prayers had been completed:

'From ghoulies and ghosties and long-legged beasties,
And things that go bump in the night,
Good Lord deliver us.'

Kenneth, meanwhile, is hovering at the edge of the circle. He frowns and fidgets. Returning with the cake and cider, the inn-keeper observes Kenneth's demeanour, and calls to him. 'Have a drink, sir. Come and sit with us beside the fire.'

But Kenneth refuses.

'You are grown men, yet you will let this creature spin you yarns, nonsensical and superstitious. Don't you know your scriptures? Let the word of God be your guide, not this irreligious claptrap! It's not fit for the ears of Christian souls.'

The old woman is not fazed by this. 'You don't know the story I have to tell, sir, so I am not sure how you know it will offend you,' she says. 'Unless you have the gift of second sight.'

'Do not insult me in this manner,' says Kenneth. 'I know only what the Maker reveals to me. There are no other portents that have any meaning.'

'Not even what is written in the stars?' asks the innkeeper.

'Heathen nonsense. Why do you want to hear old wives' tales that bring dark into a lit room and make fools of men who otherwise might sit and read the scriptures?'

'Most of us can't read them for ourselves,' says the innkeeper. 'It is different for cloisterers such as yourself.'

There is a murmur of agreement from the group.

'Let us listen to this lady, brother,' says Rowan. 'If her words are not to your taste, then go upstairs and rest. It seems that the journey has tired you — a good sleep may improve your spirits.'

'God bless you, sir, but you are not well in yourself,' says the old woman to Kenneth. 'Go to the kitchen and tell them to make up a yolk and nutmeg posset. That should settle you.'

'I shall drink nothing to *your* order!' says Kenneth.

'Brother Rowan, I suggest that we retire to our chamber. Men of the cloth do not sit at the fireside of a public inn, listening to the witless tales of crones.'

Rowan looks at the old woman. 'Please forgive my rudeness,' he says. 'And that of my brother —'

There is a 'harrumph' from Kenneth.

The old woman smiles at him. 'There will be time enough for you to hear it,' she says.

X

In the courtyard, everything is confused — Wulva can't make any sense of it. Too much light, rebounding off white walls. Too many men carrying firewood, flagons, sides of meat; and women bearing water buckets, trays of bread, or squawking chickens. Dogs of every size and shape weave among them, like river eels. The humans loom and hurry, and no one looks at her, a solitary child. She stops still, almost tripping up a boy with a dead goat slung across his back.

'What's this?' he asks. 'Can't you look where you're going?'

'I'm sorry,' she says.

'Well, be more careful.'

'I'm sorry,' she says, again.

He looks at her a little more kindly. 'Who are you with?'

'No one.'

'Have you come for the feast?'

Somehow, she is swept off, into a vast room filled with fiery heat, where she is given food, but Iochtar is shooed away. She looks up at red faces, running sweat. The scents and smells are overpowering. Waves of people hurry past, bearing platters of sizzling meat, and towering edifices she does not recognise as food. A quieter time follows, until there are only women left, clearing up the debris that remains. One stout woman nudges another. 'Who is that child?' The two stare and shrug.

'I've brought a pig,' she says. 'It's a present.'

'Oh, you will have to ask my lady about that,' says someone else. 'If it's a gift, she is the person who must receive it.'

'Who's it from?' says another.

She wonders if she can name Cailleach, Berthe, and Merrow, and decides against this. 'From me.'

The boy with the dead goat comes over and sits beside her.

'What did you say your name was?'

'Wulva.'

The boy frowns. 'Where are you from?'

'The woods.'

'What are you, the spirit of the trees? You won't get far with that queer tale. Lady Aefric has kept to her room since the bairn died.'

'A bairn?'

'Her daughter.'

'Oh.'

The two women come over and join them. 'There's a pig causing havoc in the yard,' says the first. 'Never saw that breed before.'

'He's called Iochtar,' says Wulva.

'They're from the woods,' says the boy.

The women stare. 'But whereabouts?'

'I came to give Iochtar as a present.' But Wulva would rather not give them Iochtar, nor see his throat cut, nor eat his boiled head.

'She's a puzzle, that's for certain,' says the second woman. 'There is nothing out there but heath and greenwood, nothing to live on but the land. And look at her — as bonny as the day. And that is a nice bit of cloth her gown is made from. *Someone's* had the care of her.'

The servants look at Wulva, and she looks back at them. After a while, the boy is sent to see his lordship, to tell him of the small girl and her pig.

She is taken from the hot kitchen, across the courtyard, up a flight of stairs. Here there is a quiet room with bright windows, the scent of lavender. A tall man with a red beard is sitting by the fireside in a high-backed chair.

'Is this the child?' he says. He smiles. 'Come now, speak up. Tell me, is your sole companion a pig?'

Wulva nods, not knowing what to say.

'Do you know who I am?'

'The Lord ... of something.'

He laughs at this. 'Macduff, they call me. You've baffled all my servants, Wulva — they are not used to children coming from nowhere, speaking in strange accents and claiming to know nothing of their past.'

'I didn't mean to.'

'What did you mean to do? Did someone send you? You don't seem like a villein's child, but I can't help you if you won't tell me who your people are.'

'I don't remember. I'm sorry.'

There's a sound from the far side of the room. Turning, Wulva sees that one corner is screened off, hidden by a curtain embroidered with birds and flowers.

'Ruadh? Who's there?' A woman's voice, faint and hoarse.

Macduff gets to his feet, frowning. 'There is no need to stir yourself,' he cries. 'You must rest!'

But the curtain is pulled back and a woman appears. Her hair is loose and she is wearing a nightgown.

Macduff kneels down and puts his arms around her. 'Aefric — my dearest ...'

The lady gently frees herself from his embrace. Her eyes are fixed on Wulva's face. 'Who is this? Where did she come from?'

'She is called Wulva. We know nothing more, and she is loath to tell us.'

'But ... oh ...' She stares, and her eyes fill with tears. 'Can't you see it?'

Macduff's face twists with pain. Wulva looks from him to the lady, feeling the room reel steeply and the emptiness beyond. Something presses at her chest, a grief that's not her own.

'Don't you see?' Aefric approaches Wulva. Close to, Wulva can see that her eyes are bloodshot and swollen, and can smell her sour breath. 'She is the image of poor Lorna!'

Macduff's expression changes once again. 'I don't ...' He looks from Aefric to Wulva. 'Yet ... perhaps,' he says, uncertainly. 'Yes, I can see what you are saying.'

'I'm sorry about the bairn,' says Wulva.

'She wasn't a bairn; she was a girl of nine,' says Macduff.

'About your age.' Aefric is staring at her intensely. She takes Wulva's hands and holds them tightly. 'You poor lost creature!' she cries.

After this, Wulva is taken to another chamber and given new clothes to wear. At first, she stays below, and eats at the far end of the table with the servants. But after a few days, Aefric appears at supper, and Wulva is invited to sit with the lord and lady. And so it goes on, day after day, without explanation. She becomes part of their family by small, invisible degrees, like a mushroom sprouting in the forest shade. Days become weeks and months. She stops wondering why she has been favoured in this way, and whether she really does resemble their dead Lorna. At Martinmas, they slaughter Iochtar, and she avoids eating pork on meat days for some time.

Now she learns new ways from the Macduffs, and they are not what she expected. They may be mormaers, but they are a family ruled by love and kindness. Nothing could be further from her memories of Other Beast. Aefric is quiet and gentle, and showers her attention on orphaned Wulva. She teaches her to sew, to weave, to spin; she shows her the arts of tapestry, and drawing, and how to play the harp and sing. Macduff marvels that she can read and write, and talks to her of wars and battles, of rivalry and factions. But the greatest change is wrought in her when she becomes a sister. In due course, three sons are born to Aefric: Gavin, Torin, and then Cormac. The older ones are wild and merry, growing fast, running everywhere, getting in the way, play-fighting on stairways, tending to their menagerie of creatures. But Cormac is different. He is small and slight, like a fairy child, and has wide amber eyes. He likes to roam the moor, collecting plants and birds' eggs, and has a hornbook on which he writes down words that take his fancy. 'A scholar, like his sister,' says Lord Macduff, for that is what he and Aefric have decided: Wulva, double of Lorna, has come to take her place. As for the boys, they have never known a world without their Wulva. She joins them in their games, and helps look after them, presiding over bath-time, supper, and prayers.

In the evening, they gather round the fireside, and Aefric tells them stories. The castle is full of tales, and none are thought too weird or troubling for the ears of children.

Some are brought in by troubadours and minstrels, while others are rooted in the memory of servants. No book could contain such marvels, for while the stories have a spine of repetition, containing certain elements that are thrillingly familiar, they change subtly with each telling, due to interruptions, forgotten threads, or things newly thought of by the storyteller and woven in for devilment and pleasure. These stories lurk, alive, in the children's heads, to be released on fire-lit evenings. Wulva, suckled by wolves, tutored by the sisters, finds herself more and more contented. She can still sense the forest; she can feel the fear and hunger of its creatures. Yet more and more, under the gentle eye of Aefric, she is happy in her human skin. Aefric is her guide, watching and protecting her.

Aefric teaches her the tasks that she must oversee. If others are to fulfil their duties as they must, the lady of the house must know the detail of each job, in all its precision and exactness, and what the standards are, and how to impose them without harsh words. She shows Wulva the different ways to scent the washing water — with sage, marjoram, camomile, or rosemary — and how full the bowl should be before it's brought to table. She shows her recipes for perfumes, the best way to scour with shave-grass and river sand, the use of alder leaves for catching fleas, the most efficacious use of wormwood and rue for keeping a room free of the plague. And wormwood once again, with lavender, to keep hungry moths from woollen clothes.

Wine is not merely a treat for thirsty guests — it can rescue hardened fur, as soapwort restores velvet. Wash-day is like a battle, with maidservants for soldiers. All that touches human skin takes on the human stench, if left to itself. Chemises, shirts, nightclothes, all go in the wash, while sheets and tablecloths go in the mighty buck-tub. And then there is the skill of how to make the lye, from clean wood ashes. The list seems endless, and every key on the great ring she carries at her belt has some vital purpose, in keeping something secret, separate, or safe from prying eyes.

There is as much to this as there is in the skills of witchcraft and dark magic; no scholar is called upon to use his memory more accurately. For every rule, there's an exception, and in every scheme, a flaw. Housework is a struggle against nature, but it runs according to its patterns: of daylight hours, of the seasons, of the lifespan of a salted carcase. Just as a wooden floor must be cleaned along its grain, so must a housewife know the laws of nature so as to improve on them, and keep her chambers sweet.

When Macduff is away, Wulva shares Aefric's bed, and in the deep night Aefric tells her long tales of love and yearning, a far cry from warrior stories or cautionary tales, and explains what it is she loves in Lord Macduff, and promises that one day, and soon, such a man will be found for Wulva. 'When you are ready,' she whispers. And when Aefric sleeps, gently breathing under the eiderdown, Wulva gazes up at the enclosing dark and wonders who this man will be.

This life is bright and full of laughter — though there are scoldings too, and beatings, for no caring parent spares the rod — and Wulva sometimes forgets that she does not truly belong. Sometimes she would like to become what she appears to be: a human child, a stepdaughter, the sister of three boys. Sometimes she dreams about the yew house, and the damp mystery of the woods, where tree roots bind and tangle far beneath the ground. Here, there are tree corpses beneath her feet and all around her, the grain exposed like veins. These dreams are troubled, startling.

Each spring, at Alban Eiler, Wulva goes to the oak tree at the edge of the forest, where Cailleach is waiting for her. Each time she goes, she feels a greater desire to stay at the castle, and fears that these meetings might do the Macduffs harm. She has no choice but to answer the questions that are put to her. Cailleach wants to know the name of each new bairn, and of everyone who visits the castle, from travelling minstrel to scar-faced soldier. In return, Cailleach talks about the forest and its creatures. It is a curious thing, but no matter how reluctant she may feel to meet with Cailleach, once the witch begins to spin her tale, Wulva is entranced. She feels the forest come alive around her; she recalls, though dimly, that time before the witches took her in. And each time they say goodbye, she feels something tearing, the part of her that belongs in the green dark, which can't live in the close walls of the castle. Cailleach never alters, but Wulva changes over time: taller, stronger. And also different in her heart — she loves to hear about the forest, but her yearning for it weakens as her love for the Macduffs grows and deepens. At their first meeting, she tells Cailleach all she can recall, speaking quickly, eager to be obedient. But with each passing year, her willingness is tempered by her feeling for her adopted family. She chooses her words carefully, so as to please Cailleach with as little information as she can. When the seventh spring comes, she is full grown. Pale sunlight breaks the darkness earlier each day. The harsh winds lighten. Snowdrops and hyacinths bloom in the castle gardens. Alban Eiler will soon come again.

The mirror shows a white face, dark brows, a hard and fearless gaze. Looking at her forearms, she examines the soft down on her skin. Does it grow more thickly than it should? Is she different from the other women? The curse has come, there is hair growing between her legs, and this is to be expected. That much she learned from Aefric, but there are questions that she can't put to her. Such as: if she is a mormaer, now living with her people, must she really see Cailleach again? She has lived longer here than she did with the sisters, and her time with them in the yew house seems dreamlike and ethereal, a will-o'-the-wisp in her memory. Likewise, it is hard to believe she was ever a wolf cub, though she avoids treading on the wolf pelts in the castle, and can always fancy that the great snarling heads are wakeful, watching her as she passes.

XI

Next day, Rowan is surprised to find that the old woman has departed at first light without breaking her fast.

'Not in her right mind,' says the inn-keeper. 'A lot of her sort about these days. Old age and the plague time have driven out their wits. It was an odd sort of tale she had to tell. Gave me the creeps, I don't mind telling you.'

'You were a fool for listening,' says Kenneth. 'There was the stench of Lucifer about that woman. You'd have been wiser to keep your distance.'

'I would not have missed it for all the spice in Araby,' says the inn-keeper. 'That story will stay with me till the day I die.'

Rowan can't help feeling curious. He passed a night beset by lurid nightmares: of long-jawed, ravenous wolves, kings on blood-smeared horses, a crown set on a skull.

They ride along the North Road, which follows the coastline, ascending a gently sloping hill. To the east is the blurred horizon of the sea and the outlines of distant islands. Before long they find themselves on the rugged uplands, where the wind tugs at their robes and Zeus neighs and shakes his head, as if considering a break for freedom. Kenneth retains his brooding silence, breaking it only to say prayers at the appointed times. Rowan would welcome some communication, but his years in the monastery have cured him of the need for small talk or chatter, and he is soothed by the passing scene. And as the day progresses, they encounter other travellers: a choleric farmer from Peebles, a phlegmatic prioress from the border country, a fat reeve from Dundee. For the most part, however, the road is empty, and Kenneth and Rowan proceed in silence, accompanied by the bleating of the short-tailed sheep that are grazing on the heathland, and the twittering of skylarks.

After a while, Rowan sees a dark mass to the north — a city, rising above the woods and farmland, crowning an immense grey rock. It is surrounded by a high stone wall, and surmounted by a white-towered castle. He has not seen its like before.

Kenneth reins in his horse and stares for a moment. 'Edinburgh,' he says. 'Lewd home of the Evil One.'

'Do you have a good word to say for any of the places that we pass through?'

'The sinful gather in cities, and sell their wares.'

'We are men of God! We shall turn our backs on temptation,' says Rowan. 'And in doing so, we may even set an example to our fellows.'

'You are a cloisterer to the core, and you don't know what you might encounter.'

Rowan is stung. 'I know what Mammon is, and how Satan works to foil us.'

'Ha!' says Kenneth, and kicks Zeus onward.

Edinburgh certainly smells like the haunt of sinners. When they clatter through the city gates, the stench of excrement is so powerful that Rowan gags. Kenneth, he observes, has a kerchief clutched to his mouth and nose. He thinks wistfully of the priory latrines. At least the castle might have a more wholesome aspect — Rowan looks up at the towering edifice on its jagged rock, mysterious and foreboding. Nearer to, tall buildings veer upwards, like cliffs, split by narrow streets. Clusters of faces peer down, as if the street provides their entertainment. Rowan feels dizzy and bemused. There is a rage of unfamiliar noises — the cries of street vendors and mountebanks, pipers piping, hammers banging, children yelling. Children! They are everywhere, running headlong down the streets, accompanied by barking dogs ... there is so much barking. Rowan looks around, confused. Human bodies are manifestly not designed to live like this, heaped into tall granite buildings, crowding along vertiginous alleys. He sees that the mud through which their horses are walking is in fact a thick soup containing every kind of waste and filth — fish-heads, animal entrails, floating faeces. Hestia almost stumbles in the malodorous sludge, and he sees the culprit is a sheep's head. One black eye peers up at him. Are all cities thus? He has heard talk of the filthy maelstrom that is London. A man may walk down the street there and be shat upon by his fellow, sitting in his privy up above. Purgatory must surely bear a resemblance to a city such as this.

It is some time before they reach their destination, having taken a number of wrong turnings, discovering corners of the city frequented by whores and street knaves, where lewd voices call out to them, hands grasp at their legs, and their horses snicker nervously as they proceed through the crowd. Rowan wonders what it was like before the pestilence — it is hard to imagine there being more people. Yet there must have been many deaths here.

They have now reached the edge of the city. Red clouds streak the sky; the hot afternoon is fading to dusk. Here, the narrow streets fizzle out to open ground, the road churned to mire. Large houses sit behind high walls, surrounded by orchards, a few meagre coppices of oak and pine, outposts of the old forest. At last, there is also relative quiet. A pig is being slaughtered somewhere, and making a voluble protest. Elsewhere, a boy is singing, judging by the chilling purity of the sound.

Kenneth reins in his horse outside a house that stands alone on the road, with high stone walls on each side. He takes out the parchment fragment on which the prior wrote his instructions, and looks at it.

'This is the place,' he says.

'Are you certain?' Despite the fact that night is closing in, there are no lights at the windows: the silent building has an air of melancholy. Rowan thinks with sudden longing of the wayside inn, the travellers gathered around the fire. Kenneth dismounts and bangs loudly on the door. For a while, there is no sign of life. But then the door is flung open, and a figure comes down the steps: a young man, tall and emaciated. He bows in an affected manner.

'Brother Rowan and Brother Kenneth — I have been waiting for you!' he cries. 'Father Andrew informed me of your coming, and the stars foretold the *precise* time of your arrival. The arts of prognostication have once more borne fruit.' He has a soft, sibilant voice and the appearance of a man recovering from a long illness. His face is white and somewhat swollen, his eyes bloodshot, his thin, matted hair hanging to his shoulders. His beard is so scanty that one might almost count the hairs growing from his chin. To add to the unwholesomeness of his appearance, he is wearing a long velvet robe, resembling a bishop's chasuble, embroidered with moons and figures. Despite his lack of physical grace, he is regarding the two men with an air of superiority and condescension. Supposing an owl were to take on human form — a sick, ill-favoured owl, shifty in disposition, vaunting in its opinion of itself — this Gervaise might be his double.

A servant appears and takes away the horses, and Gervaise leads them into the house. This is the reason that no lights were showing: although there are candles burning on sconces, the walls are draped with tapestries and rugs, obscuring the windows, so that the interior has the aspect of some vast oriental tent. The hangings are embroidered with exotic and unfamiliar creatures: unicorns, dragons, great worms, and numerous other curious beasts Rowan cannot name. The human figures bear horns or wear high crowns; some are on horseback. They are from the East, he suspects, having that quality of familiarity and strangeness that he associates with Persian and Hebraic texts. There are also images of the heavens, the stars and planets, embroidered in gold thread against a background of empurpled blue.

Gervaise holds his arms out, in the manner of the showman. 'I have collected some of these on my travels overseas,' he says. 'Others were gifts, sent to me by my fellow students of the arcane. In China, Constantinople, the furthest corners of the globe. Our knowledge extends like tentacles across the civilised world.'

Kenneth looks uneasy, and crosses himself. Gervaise surveys his property with a look of satisfaction. 'I know of no one with a greater collection, and these are not the only objects I have assembled over the years. You will soon see more. But I expect you are ready for supper?'

They enter a dining room with a long table, on which numerous dishes of food have been set out, and after saying their prayers and washing their hands in bowls of lustrous pewter, they proceed to eat a vast meal: brawn with mustard, mutton leg, a baked capon in a piecrust, plover in jelly, baked quince, and fruit pottage. They are also served with Rhenish and Gascon wine. Not only is Rowan surprised by the variety and luxury of the meal, he is astonished to see how much Gervaise consumes. For one so thin and sickly-looking, his appetite is prodigious. The meal is eaten in silence: Gervaise shows no sign of outward piety, but it turns out that in one aspect of his life, at least, he continues to observe the customs of a religious house. The only sounds are those of knife scraping against pewter and the (somewhat unpleasant) noise made by Gervaise chewing. Kenneth eyes his host suspiciously, and eats with concentrated deliberation. What does he make of the man? Rowan himself is puzzling over the association between Gervaise and Father Andrew. He can only assume that in his previous life, Gervaise presented a very different face to the world, for he seems far removed from the smooth, ambitious cloisterers with whom their prior habitually associates. He has about him an odour of oddball heresy that is normally anathema to a professional man of God like Father Andrew. Can it be his great wealth, as demonstrated by Gervaise's house and hospitality, that attracted him? Rowan observes his host closely. Gervaise dines with gusto and drinks almost a quart of wine, yet shows no sign of drunkenness. He is presumably used to such indulgence. It is hard to imagine him being their guide to the remote abbey, or dealing with the inevitable discomforts of a long expedition on horseback. Rowan feels unsettled and declines more wine himself. Kenneth, he observes, is less abstemious. When the table has been cleared, Gervaise gazes at his guests intensely, eyes gleaming.

'I have been looking forward to our meeting, and hope that this association will benefit us all.'

'We share that hope,' says Rowan. 'As doubtless Father Andrew has informed you, we don't know the exact location of the abbey, or what we will find there.'

'It's not easy to find, but I have a clear recollection of the route. However, it's possible you're too late. The English vandals have been there already, so word has it.' While he speaks, Gervaise's sickly face is contorted with excitement. He seems charged with an energy that's not quite human.

'I hope we haven't made a wasted journey,' says Kenneth.

'God willing, you will find at least something to your advantage when you reach the monastery,' says Gervaise. 'And no visit to this house is ever wasted. However, I prefer to speak about this in private.' He lowers his voice. 'I am careful about the servants I employ here, but some things are for the eyes and ears of gentlemen like us, rather than those of the lower kind. There are some matters beyond their ken. If you are both willing, I will escort you to my study.'

He takes up a candle and they follow him out of the hall, up a wide flight of wooden steps, and then up a corkscrew staircase. There is a closed door at the top. Gervaise takes out a bundle of keys and unlocks it. They enter a small, dark room, half visible in the guttering candle-flame. Rowan feels oppressed: there seems to be something lingering in the air he breathes — a feeling, a memory. He can't think what it is, nor why it afflicts him as it does.

'Very few people have seen this chamber — you are among the privileged elect,' says Gervaise. 'If you weren't here on Andrew's recommendation, you would not see it either. What you see around you is my mind made tactile, the tools with which I unfurl my thinking.' He lifts the candle higher, and they perceive, dimly, shakily, that the room is crowded with scientific instruments and equipment.

'What is your business here?' asks Kenneth in a hoarse voice. 'Necromancy? You know the Church's canon law condemns it. Any divination from the customs of the heathen is no more than courting the power of the Fiend. We came to you in good faith, as our guide, not to admire your occult knowledge.'

'Have no fear, brother. There is nothing here that need alarm you.'

Rowan peers around the chamber, trying to see more clearly. He is unnerved by it, and its smack of dark chicanery, and yet he knows that this may be because he is a simple man with limited horizons. The border between the sacred and the profane is not always clear. It is true that necromancy is forbidden, and summoning demons is a sin, but also true that priests sprinkle holy water on infertile fields, and he knows from his own experience that the mandrake root cures many afflictions. Yet he shares Kenneth's unease. He can't see much — vials and bulbous glass retorts and bottles containing dark liquids and unformed shapes. Books, too, and furled parchments by the dozen: sufficient texts, indeed, to form a library, though not ordered or organised to any apparent plan.

Gervaise follows his gaze. 'You are admiring my collection? There are few to rival it in Edinburgh, I believe. I have the *Leechbook* of Bald, the *Lacnunga*, and Ptolemy's *Centiloquium*, of which you may have heard.'

'Devil's work,' says Kenneth.

'Oh, Brother Kenneth, don't be so dour! Was not the birth of Our Lord attended by the Magi? Is that not an indication of a new contract between the old magic and the new? And what about the miracles that He wrought later? These were magic of a kind.'

'Your slipshod logic won't work with me,' says Kenneth. 'I was a soldier, fighting the Infidel in Spain. I know right from wrong, and I have killed for it, in God's name. I've marched two hundred miles on two days' rations. I've seen a city starved to death. I know what is and what is not, and I don't take kindly to snake-tongued quacks, nor their scholarly equivalents. Show us what you have to show us, tell us where we have to go, and let's have done.'

'Brother Kenneth, we shall not get on if you persist with

this wilful narrow-mindedness. There are more ways than your way; even the Infidel possesses valuable knowledge —'

'You speak as if there is no such thing as canon law, and the ecclesiastic condemnation of the magic you describe. The customs of the heathen are the works of Satan made manifest.'

'Really, Kenneth, please. Let us at least be cordial,' cries Rowan. But he is himself alarmed by the turn of the conversation. Gervaise, confiding and ingratiating, seems like a species of mountebank, with something sinister and injurious to sell.

Gervaise smiles patiently. 'Brother Rowan, thank you for those words. But rest assured, I am used to such reactions when I discuss my scholarship. One does sometimes feel that being of the world leads to an unfortunate myopia about what is truly significant. We live in narrow, fearful times, and run the risk of overlooking some of God's own work, mistaking it for evil. Let us be agile of mind. Let us see what might be possible, if we are open to the wisdom of the ancients.' He sets the candle down on a table, takes a small chest from beneath it, and selects another key. After unlocking the chest, he takes out a bundle of documents. 'Sit down, please,' he says, pulling out two stools. He takes a seat himself. 'Few — aside from English spies — know how to find Saint Medard's abbey. Its library contains a cache of bound volumes and precious documents, including a collection of antiquated magical texts, and certain documents about the earliest mormaer leaders and the history of the Scottish kings.' He glances at Kenneth shrewdly. 'There are also other documents there, of inestimable value. These are of great interest to me. They deal in ancient knowledge that has been lost to modern man.'

'Given that you are so familiar with the contents of the library, and the route, why have you not made the journey before?' asks Kenneth suspiciously.

'I lacked the courage,' says Gervaise. 'Since I left my order, I have been able to do as I choose. And I choose this amenable and secret darkness, and the pursuit of the studies that pique my interest. But I have long since dreamed of going to the abbey, and now that you gentlemen are making the journey, I have my chance. You will assist me, just as I am assisting you.'

Kenneth merely grunts.

Rowan has little interest in the contents of the library beyond the texts he must identify. However, it occurs to him that it might be harder than he'd first thought to ascertain that what he is copying is itself authentic. 'Who wrote the history of the Scottish kings you mention?' he asks.

'Who wrote it? Why, *monks*, of course.'

'And how do we know that they were writing down the facts? The truth?'

Gervaise gazes at him in the candlelight, perplexed. 'Why would it be otherwise? Their names fade into dust, yet they are the custodians of the facts, which they record. These were educated men, with Greek and Latin, acting in the service of Our Lord.'

Rowan doesn't know why this seems unsatisfactory. Perhaps it is the fact that he must go to such lengths to find these documents, while others have gone to such trouble to conceal them. If these were strange spells from Ur or other ancient writings, their mystery might be sufficient to convince one of their worth. But he sees, suddenly, a procession of monks just like himself, blindly copying the writings of their forebears, neither knowing the truth of any record nor caring to enquire further. He shakes his head, wishing to dispel such foolish thoughts. He casts his mind back to his conversation with Father Andrew, who is so certain that there is no matter of greater significance than the king-line of Scotland. For the prior, this embodies glory, nobility, destiny, and the recording of this information on parchment will pass down this truth to future generations. And Father Andrew thinks that there is no scribe more worthy and dispassionate than a monk, sequestered from the world, removed from the scrabbling, hubristic turmoil of secular political ambition. Rowan blinks hard and tries to think more clearly. He has a mission. He is like a knight chasing the Grail.

Gervaise unrolls a document and spreads it out before him. A faint whiff of calf-skin reaches Rowan's nostrils. 'I shall, of course, be coming with you, so there is no need to commit this route to memory,' says Gervaise. 'This is the path we shall follow. We start from here — you see? Edinburgh. Cross the Firth there. Then proceed north.' He traces with his finger. 'The abbey is beyond Loch Leven, north-east of the Monadh Ochail. The final barrier here — we must cross this mountain, there is no way to circumnavigate it. On the far side, there are joined lochs, which meet here.' He points at the neat image of a turreted building, ochre against blue. 'That is the abbey. To reach it, one must use the causeway, which is on occasion covered by water. We shall need to travel on foot for the final part of the journey. Horses are not sufficiently sure-footed. Not even mules could climb the mountain, and some men might baulk at the prospect.' He is looking at Rowan.

Rowan ignores this and peers at the signs and symbols. He has seen such charts before, but made little sense of them. He knows the wiggling, aquamarine line around the edge marks the end of the land and the beginning of the sea. It is not clear how 'Edinburgh' is meaningfully represented on the parchment. Studying this facsimile seems to make their projected journey less clear, not more so. It would make sense only if he were an ant, processing across the page.

'God willing, we shall find the place without too much difficulty,' says Kenneth, looking bored. 'I have some experience of travels to remote places myself.'

Gervaise gives another ingratiating smile. 'You are

in safe hands with me. My knowledge is more than mere orientation. When I offer advice, it is based on deep knowledge, the scholarship of the ages.'

'Oh, yes, we are aware of your great stature, never fear,' says Kenneth. 'We are humbly grateful to you for sharing this arcane knowledge with two ignorant cloisterers such as ourselves.'

'Indeed so!' cries Rowan, hoping to bring a more respectful tone into the conversation. 'I am sure it would be impossible to find the monastery without you.'

'I do not like your attitude, Brother Kenneth,' says Gervaise. 'Did the Reverend Father tell you my history, and reveal to you the wide range of my study?'

'Of course!' says Rowan. 'We have heard great things of you.'

But Kenneth has an expression of disdain. 'What I understand, for my part, is that you were a member of a religious house not unlike our own, and that you departed when your "studies" became incompatible with Christian faith. That is not a recommendation in itself, though we are not here to argue with you.'

'Each man must find his own path to God,' says Rowan earnestly.

'And each man must determine what he means by that,' says Gervaise.

Kenneth raises an eyebrow. 'The Bible is clear enough for me. We know that God is the Creator, and why we must worship Him and pray for our deliverance. It is not for us to question His nature or His essence. It is for us to try, in our humble way, to fit ourselves for the life hereafter, and to be worthy of it. We are sinners, after all, and cannot hope to reach Heaven without the forgiveness of our Maker.'

'Ha!' says Gervaise. 'Very good. Admirable piety, Brother Kenneth, estimable obedience.'

'Are you drunk, man?' asks Kenneth. 'I find your manner most unbefitting.'

Gervaise laughs outright now. 'Unbefitting? Interesting word. Clumsy in construction, obsequious in nature.'

'I have no idea what you are speaking about,' says Kenneth. 'But I smell heresy.'

'That does not surprise me. Sniffing out heretics is a large part of the business of the Church. What I am speaking of, brother, is the fact that man need not render himself stupid, dull-witted, brainless, in order to fit himself for life eternal. Man can pay his respects to the great wonders of Creation by learning about them. Here we part company, I fear, for while you smell heresy, my olfactory function detects blind obedience to creed.'

'I think, perhaps, we have all drunk our fill, and would benefit from retiring to bed,' says Rowan. 'While this discussion is intriguing, I feel that more light might be cast on these matters in the morning, over some bread and cheese.' He is glad that he refused most of the wine that Gervaise was offering, yet feels queasy and unfocused even so. His two associates are certainly the worse for drink: Kenneth is slurring.

Kenneth grunts again, and they take their leave.

XII

Cormac has another of his fevers. Sleepless during night hours, restless in the daytime, dozing fitfully, refusing food, becoming querulous and strange. Aefric diagnoses an inflammation of the blood, and gives him posset ale with violet leaves and sorrel. But only having Wulva by his side will soothe him. After six days, the crisis passes, and he takes notice of his surroundings once again. Down in the courtyard, below the window of the bedroom he shares with his brothers, there is a tiny garden, raised up from the ground like a large horse trough. It's early April, and there are daffodils growing.

'They might be lonely there,' he says. 'Trapped inside the castle.'

'But they are in the open air!' cries Wulva. 'You needn't worry about them.' She marvels at the odd way he sees the world, always making much of the smallest things, and imagining suffering where there is none.

'I think they're sad,' he says. He seems determined to feel sorry for them. 'I shall go out and find some other things, on the mountain, to keep them company.'

Aefric says that it will do him good to walk in the fresh air. She holds him gently, and strokes his hair. So it is agreed that Wulva will take him out, though not too far. They follow a rugged pathway that leads from the castle to a ridge of moorland, going hand in hand. The path is rough and stony and passes beside a loch. Despite the brightness of the day, the water is slate-grey. Sluggish waves suck gently at the shingle. A solitary crow flaps slowly overhead. When they see the yellow gorse-bushes blooming on the mountainside, Cormac flushes with excitement.

'The sun has landed!' he shouts, letting go of Wulva's hand and running into the gorse. 'The mountain's caught the sun! See? It reached up, when the snow had melted, and caught hold of a bit of golden, and then pulled it down. Look! Look at it!'

She can only laugh and follow him, the thorns pricking her skin. It seems a shame to put him right, and the sight is indeed so wonderful that she could easily believe there was magic in it. He runs hither and thither, collecting little things he finds among the gorse-bushes. As she watches him, she makes a promise to herself: that she will sever her connection with the witches, that she will stay with the Macduffs, and live as ordinary people do, and share their lives as if she never knew another way.

He comes back and shows her his collection: a white stone, like a giant pearl; a bird's egg, blue as sky; an empty snail-shell; and a tiny skull, no bigger than a fingertip.

'What is it?' he asks.

'A shrew, I think,' says Wulva. 'Or perhaps a vole.'

'A baby?'

'It might be.'

'That never lived?'

'Well, it lived once. A little time, maybe.'

'Oh.' He looks at the tiny thing, held in Wulva's palm. 'I don't think I want to put these treasures in my garden,' he says.

'No? Not to keep the flowers company?'

'No. Because they're born out here. I shall find a place, and make a grave where it is cold and windy, which is what they know.'

So they find a flat stone, up on the ridge, and he arranges his treasures in a circle, like a sort of diadem. 'Will they blow away?' he asks.

If it had been the other boys, Wulva might have told a half-truth, as one does to satisfy a child. But there is a quality in Cormac that makes it impossible to tell him anything but what you really know. 'They might,' she says. 'It's not very sheltered.'

He seems satisfied with that. 'They'll be here for a while,' he says.

They turn back, and retrace their steps along the side of the loch. The weather has suddenly shifted, as it often does on the mountain, and clouds blot out the sun. A cold blast of wind tears at Wulva's hair, whipping it across her face.

The waters shudder, and rain falls heavily.

They half walk, half run, stumbling on the path, which is already soaked and slippery. There's a lightning flash and then a clap of thunder. It sounds as if the sky is being ripped apart by monsters. Cormac screams and tears his hand from hers, runs ahead, skidding and slipping.

'Cormac! Be careful!'

He pays no attention. Another flash of lightning and then, almost in the same instant, a roll of deafening thunder. The storm is overhead. She puts her head down and runs as fast as she can. 'Cormac! Wait!' she cries.

But suddenly, he trips. She hears him scream, then, horribly, the sound ends in silence. When she reaches him, she takes him in her arms. He has been knocked unconscious. She gets to her feet to find her way is blocked by a cloaked and hooded figure.

'The child is hurt, please, let me by,' she says, gabbling, unthinking. 'I must get home to his mother.'

'*His* mother,' says the figure. 'As you say. There seems to have been a lack of understanding in that sphere. Some blurring of the facts.'

It is Cailleach, taller, colder than she has seemed before. Her hood falls back and her face is impassive.

'Cailleach, what devilry is this?' Wulva asks. 'Do you haunt me like a spirit?'

'Alban Eiler has been and gone, and there was no one at the tree.'

'What do I care for that? The child is hurt; let me past so I can help him!'

'If you do not have a care now, you will regret it in the future. You made a bargain with us, and you must stick to it.'

'I don't remember having much say in the matter. You found me, and you used me, and you seek to use me still.' But she knows that she should not have crossed the witches.

'We saved you,' hisses Cailleach. 'We succoured you. We trained you and made you wise. Without us, your bleached bones would be all that's left of you. We saved you, and then we made you. And yet you fail to honour our agreement.'

'Forgive me,' says Wulva, close to tears.

'I told you, did I not, that the hour would come when all would be revealed to you? That time is now.' Cailleach takes her arm. 'Listen carefully to what I have to say. You will know what to do when the moment comes. You are a woman now. You are aware of what that signifies?'

She thinks of Aefric and Lord Macduff, and of her woman's curse-blood. 'Yes.'

'The Macduffs will receive a guest. You will mark him, and flatter him, and make him believe he is your master.'

She winces. 'People are always coming to the castle. There are always men.'

'You will know him when you see him. Likewise, he'll know you.'

'*How* will I know him?'

'Just remember what I've told you.'

'But —'

'Do not "but" me when you have already betrayed me! You have no choice in this; you must do what I command. Remember all you've learned about the mormaer-world, and the evil that it's done.'

'They have been kind. They've treated me as their own child.' Cormac stirs in her arms, and she glances at him anxiously.

'But you are no such thing. You are a changeling. We sent you there for a good reason. Sentiment will not assist you — the time of learning is now done.'

Her heart quails. She holds Cormac more tightly. 'What will you have me do?'

Wulva sees, then, that Cailleach is not alone. Berthe and Merrow have also appeared. The stench of sour milk emanates from swollen, clumsy Berthe, while half-translucent Merrow stinks of fish. And it is Merrow who comes towards Wulva, silver scales falling onto the wet ground.

Closer, closer, closer, till they are lip to lip — and she kisses Wulva, and her scaled tongue tastes of lust.

Cormac soon recovers. But there is not much respite before the witch's prophecy comes to pass. A few days later, Wulva hears that there is to be a great feast, to greet a new arrival. A mormaer from the north is coming with his men. They are to hunt boar, and there are to be celebrations. Such is the chaos and frenzied activity that for a while she is caught up in the preparations. But then Aefric takes her to one side.

'When our guest comes ...' She looks at Wulva, uncertain. 'My lord Macduff has asked that you entertain our visitor. His wife died, not long ago.'

'I shall do as my lord says.'

'But yet — I don't know.' Aefric frowns. 'You are so young. Be careful. Talk to him only in company. If anything disturbs you, come to me. You are our daughter, and only just a woman.'

'Who is this guest? What is his name?'

'Lord Macbeth,' says Aefric. 'A great warrior.' She hesitates then lowers her voice. 'My lord thinks very well of him as a soldier. But I do not admire him as a man. He is the sort that is never still, never satisfied. Even in the firelight, when there's talk and laughter, you can see him looking outward, at the dark. He's ... greedy, hungry. *Cruel.* Even his love of hunting is greater than it should be. There are no more boar living in his country, which is why he has journeyed here.'

'Are you afraid of him?'

Aefric takes her hands. 'My child, there is only so much I can tell you. This is a matter of allegiance, and what will come I cannot say.' Her voice drops to a whisper. 'Be careful of him. Be guarded. And don't repeat this. What I have said must go no further.'

Wulva goes to her chamber and closes the door. She thinks of the witches and their mission. Standing at the window, she watches the stormy clouds. Then she takes her finest clothes from the chest and lays them on the bed. A bodice trimmed with fur and silver thread, broadcloth skirts of deepest scarlet.

He arrives, in the midst of other men. Glittering, black-haired, wolf-pelts around his shoulders. His eyes are pale, and when their gaze meets, she feels a jerk, a shock. *It's you.* She knows that face, she knows that scent. He bows his head, watching her intently. She feels his presence like a fever, cold and hot at the same time. The sickness presses down on her. Is this part of their spell? *No good can come of this*, she thinks, but she cannot tear her eyes away.

Macduff calls her over; they talk of wars, of kings, and plans for battle. They talk of horses, plunder, areas for expansion. There is worthless land — mountains, chiefly — and land worth dying for. This is the land that may be fenced and ploughed and cultivated. Blood for food, food for blood. Macduff glances at her; she knows he wants her to say something to impress his guest, but the moment passes, and she remains dumb. This does not seem to matter. The talk shifts to the boar-hunt, and the plans for the following day. There's a wide forest on the mountainside where boar are still plentiful. All the while, Macbeth is watching her, and there has never been a watching like it. She feels as if she is under the eye of Almighty God, or maybe the eye of Satan. Her body and her face are charged with a power beyond her understanding, and within that power she's nothingness, a puff of sky.

'Why are you so quiet?' he asks, the talk around them vanishing.

'Why should I speak?'

He touches her forehead. 'There is much in here. I see it.'

She feels as if she is standing on the edge of a steep cliff, as if the drop is all around her, as if she dare not take a step. If there's a task to do, an errand to run, she cannot name it. All there is in all Creation is this: a finger held out, touching her skin; beneath the skin, the bone.

'Wulva,' he says, considering. 'A curious sort of name. And you are a curious kind of creature, aren't you? Not quite what you seem.'

And she thinks of what Cailleach said: *You will know him when you see him. Likewise, he'll know you.*

There is a storm brewing beyond the castle walls; the sky is reeling, and the three sisters are out there, riding the steep winds, making a pattern of what is yet to come, spinning cloud into frenzy. Sea-scapes mount into the night sky and crash down upon the splintered ships below.

The down on her arms itches. She drinks a cup of wine, and he notes her every move. There is no escaping this; she cannot get away. White flesh in a red gown, heart beating like a drum.

XIII

Rowan wakes for Matins feeling thirsty and sweaty. Kenneth is lying stretched out beside him, deeply asleep, his mouth open, drooling. Too much wine, yes. It looks as if he will be missing his night-prayers for once. Rowan does not have the heart to waken him. Let him sleep on! The evening was a queer one; he feels uneasy when he thinks about Gervaise, their new travelling companion. Indeed, so unsavoury is this prospect that he feels more warmly towards the austere Kenneth than he would have thought possible. He begins to say his prayers — the thirtieth psalm is an apt choice.

> *I will extol thee, O Lord, for thou hast lifted me up,*
> *And hast not made my foes to rejoice over me,*
> *O Lord my God, I cried unto thee, and thou hast healed me,*
> *O Lord, thou hast brought up my soul from the grave:*
>
> *Thou has kept me alive, that I should not go*

down to the pit
Sing unto the Lord, O ye saints of his,
And give thanks at the remembrance of his holiness,

For his anger endureth but a moment;
In his favour is life: weeping may endure for a night,
But joy cometh in the morning.

But then he breaks off. Did he hear a sound? A man, crying out? He stops, listens. Perhaps one of the servants has risen early. At first he hears nothing more; the house is still. Something pricks his curiosity, however. There was a strange quality to the sound he heard, something odd. He goes to the door, steps out onto the dark landing, and listens again. Then he hears a deep groan, raw and guttural. Someone must be hurt — perhaps he can help them? But supposing — he tries to form the thought without self-defilement — supposing it's the sound of sexual congress, with which he is so unfamiliar? It might be safer to go back to bed. He is about to slip back into his chamber, but then he hears the sound a third time, and it chills his blood. A long, agonising scream. This is not the sound of fornication: some poor creature is suffering horribly.

Walking quietly, he crosses the landing, following the direction of the cries. They come, he realises, from downstairs. He descends the staircase into the great hall, and the noise grows clearer. But still, it comes from below. At the back of the hall, a narrow flight of steps leads down to a cellar door. Unmistakeably, this is where the sounds are coming from. Rowan pauses before opening the door, scared of what might lie behind it. When he does push it open, he realises he was right to be afraid.

In the dim candlelight, he sees a tall figure in a magician's robe, which he knows to be Gervaise, though his face is turned away. Beyond him, squatting on the floor, is a creature so hideous that Rowan can hardly believe it is not a fiend from nightmare. In form, shape, size, it is a pig — more exactly, a great hog, dark and bristled. But where there should be the snouted head of the low beast, there is the face of a man — as hog-like a man as can be imagined, but a man, nonetheless. And in place of forelegs and pigs' trotters, there are human hands. Rowan screams, and Gervaise spins round, his face twisted with rage.

'What is the meaning of this? How dare you invade this private sanctum?'

At first Rowan struggles to speak, and can only stare in horror at the creature. 'How is this ... possible?' he says, at last. *'What is it?* I can scarce believe my eyes! Does it have *life?'*

'None of your concern! Get out!' Advancing, Gervaise attempts to push Rowan out of the room.

Rowan struggles to free himself. 'I beg to disagree, sir!

Any Christian man would wish to intervene, to pray for this poor creature, and for you!' They are entwined for a moment, battling with each other. Rowan manages to shriek: 'This is cruellest heresy!'

Gervaise gives him an almighty shove. 'Get out, get out!'

But they are interrupted by the pig-man, wailing: 'Hulp!' Or perhaps it belches. 'Hulp,' it says again. 'Gud mercy.' A new horror comes upon Rowan — that the thing is partly sentient, knows itself to be a man, although it's just a monstrous copy. He is reeling, attempting not to vomit up his gorge, and clings vainly to the hope that this is indeed a foul, unnatural dream, from which he will soon awaken. But nothing about his present experience has the quality of nightmare; it is all too solid.

'Quiet, you fool,' cries Gervaise, twisting round to address his prisoner. 'Do you not see what you have done, with your mindless bellowing? If the world finds you, they will put you in a fair! If the Church finds you, they will string you up!'

Kenneth appears, bleary-eyed and staggering slightly. Pushing his way in front of Rowan, he stares wildly at the scene. 'In God's name, what is this?' he cries. 'What madness is afoot?'

'You gentlemen are witness to an aspect of my skill,' says Gervaise, trying to recover his composure. 'A living experiment, you may call it. I am a man before my time.'

'Is it a trick?' asks Kenneth. 'Are you playing false with us? If so, it's a cruel and wicked subterfuge. We can pay to go inside a mountebank's tent if we want to see such things.'

'No trick! This is wrought by scientific knowledge. I have studied at the universities of Bologna and Salerno, and correspond with the most learned men in Christendom. There is nothing elsewhere to rival this discovery.'

'But it isn't possible!' says Rowan. 'This person ... this thing ... does not exist in nature. It cannot be.'

'I assure you, through my skill I have made it so. Through study, and perseverance, and the application of the knowledge of the ancients, I have created something novel, unknown in the natural order. A hybrid, something like a mule, but more ingenious, with greater utility. A man's mind given porcine context, capable of heavy work and independent thinking.'

'Foul, demonic blasphemy! The ability to create life is the province of the Maker and only the Maker,' says Kenneth. He makes a sudden movement, and Rowan sees something glitter in his hand.

'There is no need to wield your knife, brother!' he cries, alarmed. 'You are not crusading now!'

Kenneth ignores him. 'There is a special place in Hell for men like you,' he says to Gervaise. 'Whose sin goes far beyond the evil of which ordinary mortals are capable. Who spend their lives perverting what is right and just and God-given, and making it pernicious.'

'You speak of Hell, but your philosophy is for lesser men than me,' says Gervaise, eyeing the blade. 'I have superseded any understanding you can aspire to, and such mean obedience is not for me. No man has done what I have done, and will not do so for a thousand years. I bred him, I made him, I gave him life. I plucked his body from the dam, and oversaw her suckling him. Old wives speak of such creatures, but here is one in full view, not mired in some hag's tale. Here is a living miracle, not God-given, no, but glorying His name, nonetheless, using the gifts that I was born with. This is the fruit of human vision.'

'A fucking monster,' says Kenneth. The monk has gone; he is the soldier now. 'That is your triumph. You have made a cursed freak!'

'Gud mercy! Agh, Gud mercy un ma,' screams the creature.

Rowan tries to speak, but his throat is filling with bile. He looks at the creature, sees its wild pig-eyes, and is filled with terrible sorrow.

Kenneth has no such difficulty. In a resounding voice, he cries: 'Banish from me all spells, witchcraft, black magic, evil spells, ties, curses, and the evil eye; diabolic infestations, oppressions, possessions; all that is evil and sinful, jealousy, deceitfulness, envy; physical, psychological, moral, spiritual, and diabolical ailments.'

His voice fills the small room, the words seeming bigger than the space they occupy. 'Burn all these evils in Hell, that they may never again touch me or any other creature in the entire world. I command and bid all the powers who molest me — by the power of God all-powerful, in the name of Jesus Christ our Saviour.'

'Do not dare address me in this fashion!' Gervaise takes a step towards Kenneth, raising his hands.

But Kenneth is implacable. 'Through the intercession of the Immaculate Virgin Mary — to leave me forever, and to be consigned into the everlasting Hell where they will be —'

'How dare you use the words of the Exorcism against me, sir! How dare you come into my house, accept my hospitality, seek my advice, and —'

The knife flashes in the candlelight as the pig-man's screams grow louder. All is confusion, bodies, grabbing hands and punching fists. Rowan falls to the ground. 'For pity's sake!' he cries, trying to get to his feet, but slips in a sticky pool, which smells of blood. He crawls towards the door, blinded with terror, but there is something in the way that writhes and twitches. There is chaos, more shouting. Another scream, piercing, horrible. Rowan claps his hands to his ears, but the screaming will not stop.

Somehow, he is on his feet. Gervaise is sitting in a pool of blood, half conscious. Kenneth is standing over him, knife in hand. The creature is lying at his feet, bleeding. Its throat has been cut so violently that the head is almost severed. Rowan throws himself across the room, using strength he didn't realise he still possesses, and grabs hold of Kenneth.

'That is enough! Stop this foul violence immediately! What are you thinking of? Remember who you are!'

Caught off guard, Kenneth drops the knife, and Rowan seizes it.

'By God, you will pay for this!' says Gervaise, thickly. He cranes his head up to look at Kenneth. There is blood splashed across his face. 'You will be hearing from the Justiciar! I shall take you to the assembly; I shall see you hang.'

Kenneth collects himself, wipes his hand across his mouth. 'I doubt very much that you will be informing anyone of anything. I have merely slaughtered a pig, and I see no butchers hang for that particular offence. As to any injury I've done to you, I suggest that you further consider what you have been up to here, in this hellish little fiefdom of yours. Necromancy is a crime, and it is you who will be punished, not I, if you report this. For myself, I only regret that I did not kill you too, as a just punishment for this vile heresy. And I would have done so, had it not been for Rowan's soft heart.'

'He was not a pig; he was a newly minted man,' says Gervaise. Tears are pouring down his face. 'Look at his hands.'

And indeed, when he looks closer, Rowan sees how humanlike they are: perfect white hands, with small, neat nails. The face, too, seems more fully human now he sees it clearly, its eyes wide open, filled with horror, its mouth distorted by its final scream.

'You are not a *meat-butcher*,' says Gervaise. 'This was a man.'

'A monster, more like!' cries Kenneth. But he has a desperate look about him.

Gervaise is sobbing freely now, his tears mixing with his flowing blood. 'Even if you evade temporal punishment, you will take your knowledge of this murder to the grave.'

XIV

The hunters are cantering along the drove-way. A great posse of them, an invading army come to lay waste to the forest. There are spears, pennants, a pack of hounds: catch-dogs, bay-dogs, and straining, muzzled alaunts, greatest and most savage of all canines, which will as readily eviscerate a man as they will kill a boar. Macduff is in the lead. To the rear, Wulva rides a wilful grey that belongs to Aefric. The mare tosses her head, excited to be out. The wind is up, wet gusts tugging at Wulva's cloak. All her energies are concentrated on keeping in her seat, and restraining her mount from leaping forward in full gallop. She's nervous of the horse, and how the day might be.

The first thing she heard this morning was a subdued quarrel on the stairs.

'*Why* should she go with you?' This was Aefric.

'He has asked me. And he's our guest.' Macduff's voice now.

'It is no place for a woman! And she's barely that.'

'She will be safe. I shall be with her.'

'You have dominion over wild beasts, now, do you?

Those hogs are like the Devil when they are roused.'

'Be silent and do as you are bidden. It is not for me to cross our guest, nor for you to question my decision.'

'You know what kind of man he is. And yet you seek to please him.'

It is so unlike Macduff and Aefric to argue that the exchange seemed shocking. When the command came for Wulva to join the hunting party, Aefric kept out of the way. As they clattered out of the courtyard, Wulva saw her watching from an upper window, and raised her hand. But Aefric did not respond.

The mare is distracted, whinnying and prancing instead of keeping pace with the others. Ahead, one of the horsemen detaches from the rest, turns, and comes cantering towards her. She sees that it's Macbeth. He doesn't stop until his horse is close to hers, and she can see his face clearly. In the daylight, it is lined and weather-beaten. His pale, glittering eyes are fixed on her as if she were the prey. He's older than she realised, and thinner. But she sees nothing weak in him, only fierce purpose. He leans forward, and speaks urgently. 'What's this? This lagging behind? This is no place to dawdle. You must be alert. And *keep up.*'

She winces, as if she's touched a burning skillet. Accustomed to the kindness of the Macduffs, the harshness of his manner excites her. She wishes she knew how to hurt him, or cause him sorrow.

'Can't you speak?' he says. 'I never met a maid so dumb.'

'I can speak when I am minded to,' she says, firmly. 'Or when it's needed.'

He laughs, and wheels round until his horse is facing the same way. 'We shall ride together, and you will do as I do. Understood? If there is danger, you will be safe with me. See?' He shows her his hunting spear. The silver head shines in the subdued light.

'I have this,' she says. She shows him the dagger on her belt.

'I would not like to see a woman close enough to any boar to use that toy. And now — kick your beast on. Put some mettle in it. We need to make more speed.'

Soon, they enter the great forest. She has not been this way before. It is not her woodland, not the place she knew before she came to the Macduff castle, and she's baffled and unnerved by the difference she finds here, riding amid men and hunting dogs. She's on the outside, even though once the hounds have a scent, they crash off the path and veer into the trees, stumbling over brambles and fallen logs. All is dark, and outward, bark and thistle, briar and thicket, the shrieks of birds in flight. The deeper in they go, the greater her sense that the forest turns its back on them, so the shouting men and barking dogs are more and more alone and separate. She's hunted before, with Macduff and his steward, and their hunting is quiet and stealthy. A creature is located, watched, and stalked with patience and cunning. They learn to understand the beast before they take its life — following its paths, marking its habits. But this is different; this is an assault upon the woods.

The hounds catch a scent, and the hunters crash along behind them, their horses jumping fallen logs and leaping over streams. Then the scent is lost, and the hounds go snuffling this way, that way, seeking another. The riders proceed slowly now, between thickly growing trees. All around her, Wulva feels the presence of the woodland creatures, and the others who live here: demons, banshees, trolls. The watchers who keep note of what the mormaers do, who settle up when they are ready. She wishes she dared break away and ride back to the castle, but her fear of the journey back is greater than her fear of staying with the men. Nor does she know if she *could* slip away — Macbeth's gaze is on her, always, even as he talks to the hunters, chastises his dogs, rails against lack of progress. Then, suddenly, they are off again, horns blowing, dogs barking, helter-skelter through the crashing trees. Somewhere ahead, she hears the grunting and squealing of boars — it sounds as if they are chasing a herd. She can't see far, all is green confusion. The mare stumbles and Macbeth is there, catching the bridle. As he reaches forward, she sees the white skin of his arm, striped with scarlet, and wonders who or what has wounded him. He leans across and whispers 'Stay by me. We'll have this brute.' She smells his fresh sweat; her senses whirl and swim.

Then she hears it, a roar, coming from behind them,

monstrous, a squeal of purest anger, hoof-beats, a great black beast, head down, running headlong towards the mare. The horse screams and wheels round, and Wulva loses her balance, falls to the thudding ground, rolls to one side. She's confused, stunned, as afraid of being trampled by her own horse as she is of the raging boar. The mare rears up, the world tips; there's scarlet, screaming, something knocks her. Then there is a savage cry, a whir of cold above her head, a terrible, guttural scream of pain and fury. Something falls, there's the sudden stench of blood, and she is splattered with warm fluid. She's lifted, she's on a horse, but not her own. Confused, she tries to take the reins, but other hands are on them. There is a man behind her; his breath is on her neck.

Macbeth is whispering in her ear. 'Blooded, well blooded; you should be proud. Don't wipe that off, or you will bring ill luck. Let it dry and praise God the beast is dead.'

The boar is lying on its side, its mouth open in its last scream. Macbeth reaches down and pulls out the spear that's embedded in the creature's head. He regards the bloodied weapon. 'Never missed my mark yet, nor do I expect I ever will.'

There is great celebration when they return to the castle, great noise and feasting. Roast meats, skewered pheasant, mutton pies, fruit tarts, and honey-soaked pastries. Macbeth does not at first relinquish her, but keeps her close beside him, boasting of his prowess, making her show everyone her crusted, bloodied face. The truth is that she does not want to leave him; there is a heat rising in her that she feels might drive her mad. Then the drink flows, they are uncoupled, she is lost in crowds of women, Aefric is telling her to eat. She makes her excuses early, goes up to her empty chamber. It is cold after the hot room, but it cannot cool her longing.

Alone, she lies awake, waiting to hear his tread. Utterly fixed on what she wants to have. But then she sleeps, and dreams she's flying. The world spins on her wing — mountain crags, elderwood, the wintry sea. She dives and brings the forest close, stark branches clawing upwards, below them tangled dark. A creature, black and lithe, hurtling through the undergrowth. Then she's emerging from a hollow tree. Everything is bright and frozen. Going down on all fours, she sniffs the ground then prowls across the clearing, black paws marking the white ground. Dead boar gore-smeared, entrails flowing from its belly. Tears at the creature's flesh, pulls it from the bone, gobbling and dribbling as she chews the meat. Squats back on her haunches. Blood is running down her chin.

Then the room is full of light, and Cormac is sitting on the bed, asking questions. Why is your face so dirty? Why have you been playing in the mud? She wipes her face clean, daren't look in the glass. Her teeth feel sharp, she's nauseous. She feels Macbeth has shunned her — that she offered herself wordlessly, and he saw fit to stay away.

XV

Black clouds crown the mountains up ahead, ominous and brooding. They fill their water bottles at a well, but neither man wants to eat. Although they passed several pie-stalls near the city gates, the smell of them made Rowan feel as if he might throw up. His sole aim is to put as much physical distance as possible between himself and the ugly and violent scenes he witnessed. Is Gervaise possessed? Has Satan prompted his wickedness? Rowan's memory of the encounter is blurred and incomplete. Looking at Kenneth's bloodstained habit and cold face, he knows it was a true event. The facts and the horror go round and round his head. It is the strangeness that most afflicts him, its queerness. None of this has a place in the universe he understands.

Man's knowledge does not encompass the whole of God's Creation: the world contains creatures beyond human knowledge and understanding. Great Worms inhabit lochs and forests, sailors are beguiled by sea-nymphs, and the common eel, the staple of a villein's table, is birthed like magic from mud. Besides, who is he to say what *is* and what *is not*? His body is impaired by sickness, and sound is often blurred and distorted. His sight, it is true, has so far seemed unaffected, but it's possible that his senses have misled him. He wonders, again and again, if he might have imagined the whole scene, or dreamed it. Round and round his mind goes. What can be truly known? What remains mysterious? Nothing is in its right place, the world is upside-down. He sees a horrid vastness: God below, the Devil above, angelic hosts rising eel-like from the clay, and Gervaise a pious Christian. He is confused, feels poisoned, can still smell the strange perfume that filled Gervaise's house. Now that there is no question of Gervaise being their guide, Rowan does not know how they will find the abbey. The two men have not discussed this. Indeed, they have barely spoken since saddling up their mounts before daybreak.

They ride for hours, in silence, paying a ferryman to take them across the Firth — a crossing made difficult by their nervous horses — then travelling across a green and rolling landscape, with the sea to their east and a range of blue hills to the west. The ferryman confirms that they must travel north, towards Loch Leven. The hills must be the Monadh Ochail. If Rowan had known that they would be travelling without Gervaise, he would have paid more heed to what was said about their route. As it is, they are in the hands of God. There is no question of discussing this with Kenneth, who is humped morosely in his saddle, not saying a word.

They journey at a steady pace. The weather is cool for the

time of year, and there is a light drizzle from time to time. Rowan realises that despite his anxiety and discomfort, he finds riding easier now. Despite his troubled thoughts, his bodily health is better now than it was in the abbey. The damp, inclement weather soothes him; he is glad they are not proceeding in bright sun. Hours pass, and they stop only to fill their drinking horns at a well and to buy bread at a wayside village. After a while, he notices that the sun is low in the sky, and the light is fading. A blackbird sends its warning call, and he sees a fox crossing the path ahead. They descend into a valley. There is a stream, splashing over rocks, and the wet ground sucks at the horses' hooves. Each step sags and squelches. Greenwood trees are clustered near the stream, the smell is dank, and midges dance upon the water.

'Do you know where we are?' he calls to Kenneth, now slumped so low that he might already be sleeping.

Kenneth does not turn round. 'No.'

'Do you see any sign of habitation?'

'No.'

'We must find a place to rest by nightfall.'

'At nightfall, we shall sleep wherever we find ourselves. God will be our protector.'

They ride on until the light begins to fail, leaving the valley for the rocky uplands, where the wind is chilly and the curlews cry. The only trees for miles are low and stunted, bent double like cowed villeins. At length, they come to a place where the land is flatter, covered in springy turf.

'This will do,' says Kenneth.

They unroll their spare tunics and spread them on the ground, which is mercifully dry. The horses roam around peaceably, nibbling the turf, and Rowan almost envies them: indifferent to geography and fond of eating grass.

Next day, it starts to rain. They mount up and ride on, now seeing little but the path before them. A cloud descends in the middle of the morning, so they proceed in dense fog. The drove-way is their only guide — a rough track following a line of higher ground — but this is now muddy and slippery, and the horses trip and stumble. Kenneth rides ahead, still silent, and Rowan's discomfort grows as the day goes on. The path may lead anywhere; they have nothing by which to orientate themselves, not even the distant line of hills.

He can prevaricate no longer. 'Kenneth, are you certain that we are going in the right direction?'

'Yes.'

'I'm pleased to hear that, but nonetheless. The path seems to be fizzling out, and while I am sure those mountains are those to which Gervaise referred —'

'Could you refrain from mentioning that cursed blasphemer's name again? There is no need for it.'

'Of course, but let us keep a sense of proportion. It is essential that we follow the correct path, is it not, and without him to guide us —'

'He would have been quite useless.'

'Well, that may be true, but going the wrong way will cost us days at least, and these are wild places. One might be lost for weeks —'

'I've seen wilder. Around Granada, there are deserts and mountains for hundreds of miles, and wolves and boars the size of lions. Don't fret so; you are like an old woman.'

Rowan looks around, but there is nothing to see but fog and rain. 'You are the soldier, and I bow to your superior knowledge, but I would still like some reassurance. Are we just proceeding in ignorance? In the hope that we will find the way? Or do you have a clearer picture?'

'You saw the map yourself. We are heading north, aren't we? Be patient, brother, and at your ease. God will guide us.'

When night draws in again, and all they have to eat is a hunk of stale bread, Rowan feels even more dejected.

'Might we not catch a squirrel or something for the pot?' he asks. 'I am sorely hungry.'

'It's too wet to make a fire,' says Kenneth, dismissively. 'Let us say the paternoster.'

Rowan passes a sleepless, shivering night, and sends up his own self-interested prayers: for deliverance, a warm bed, and a hot meal.

His prayers are answered after a fashion. Late the next morning, they meet a goat-herd. A skinny young boy with pale blue eyes and a harelip, he has barely more conversation than his charges. He shares his food with them, eyeing them cautiously, while his wise-looking terrier gnaws a bone. The food is not hot, but it is sustaining — a slice of haggis. When the boy does speak, his impairment makes his words barely intelligible.

'Simple-minded,' says Kenneth, under his breath.

'Nonsense,' mutters Rowan in reply. 'Poor unfortunate boy.'

'I should say his dog is sharper.'

'Hush.'

'Is this the way to Saint Medard's?' enquires Rowan after they have eaten, avoiding Kenneth's eye.

The boy stares blankly at him.

'An abbey,' says Rowan. He searches his memory. 'Between two lochs.'

The boy shrugs again.

'Abaid,' says Kenneth. Picking up a broken stick from the ground, he draws the outline of two lochs in the mud, and between them the outline of a dwelling. He points to it. 'Abaid,' he says again.

'Lost,' says Rowan. 'Air chall.'

'Hardly that,' says Kenneth. 'Merely seeking confirmation.'

The boy smiles at last, his ruined mouth looking suddenly beautiful. Leaning forward, he draws his own picture, a mountain in front of the joined lochs. Then he gets to his feet, and points to the outline of a mountain on the skyline, dark against the rainy sky. Rowan nods enthusiastically, praying that they are indeed going the right way. They continue together, and he is heartened by the company of the goat-boy and his herd. The sound of curlews merges with the gentle ringing of their bells.

The mist has cleared, though the rain continues, and as they ride beside a rushing stream, Rowan studies the wild and rugged scene, the stark hills, and the purple heathland. Black clouds pile the sky, seeming as solid as the rocks below. He feels more hopeful, but then his thoughts turn to the task in prospect, and his nagging certainty that he is not the right man for the job. The problem with men of great confidence, like Father Andrew, is that they sweep all obstacles before them. They are men of action. An admirable quality, much vaunted, but such men are not good listeners. The Reverend Father confuses the strength of his own opinions with veracity, the truth. In this case, the truth was that Rowan should have stayed in the monastery, tending herbs. Even in his prime, his skill had been in making a good copy, forming a perfect letter. Later, due to shortages of labour which predated the pestilence, he had learned the craft of inking wondrous creatures along the margins. He had derived great satisfaction from crafting the facsimile of a running stag or sometimes a more fanciful creature, should the text allow. His unicorns were exemplary. For some reason, he preferred them blue.

He looks up at the landscape ahead, which is steepening. Sparse grass is giving way to naked rock. The boy comes to a halt and his goats wander on, grazing and jangling. He points to the horizon, and there, through the drizzle, they see the outline of the mountain.

'Is the abbey on the other side?' asks Rowan.

The boy nods. He raises his arm in farewell, and whistles for his dog.

They press on, amid rocks and boulders, the horses proceeding slowly. Each time Rowan believes they have reached the highest point, another horizon comes up ahead, higher up, and the way becomes more rugged and precipitous. It is late in the day when they reach the foot of the mountain, and they are obliged to pass the night there. Next day, Kenneth declares, almost with satisfaction, that it is time to leave the horses behind. With a heavy heart, Rowan relieves Hestia of her pack, and removes her saddle and bridle. She has become a dear friend, though not always a cooperative one.

'It is a great extravagance, don't you think? Turning them free?' he says to Kenneth. 'And how are we supposed to make the return journey?'

'Father Andrew knew he was unlikely to see those beasts again,' says Kenneth, implacably. 'He has included their loss in his fiscal planning, you may be sure of that. And as for our return journey, if God is willing, we shall walk, as pilgrims do. I for one will rejoice in any hardship we encounter.' This is the longest speech he has made since they left Edinburgh.

They begin the ascent. For the next few hours, Rowan's thoughts are centred on his survival. The cliff becomes steeper and more intractable as they go. There are some sections where it is possible to walk upright, more or less, though sometimes he misses his footing and stumbles. But there are also sections of sheer rock. These must be climbed. It is often difficult to find a handhold, as not all the rocks are securely embedded. The higher they climb, the colder it gets, and Rowan begins to tremble. His limbs threaten to convulse, like those of the dying, as if his body senses death even though he is yet to fall. He does not look down; his entire self is wedded to the challenge of not doing so. He looks upward, upward, towards the cliff top and his Maker. But his body senses the great void, his bowels sense it — he is but a feeble man. As he grasps blindly for something to grab hold of, he thinks of Christ's agony. 'The spirit is willing but the flesh is weak.' In the great panoply of men, lined up in their thousands, millions possibly, stretching back to Roman times and further back, the Greeks, there can have been few men with flesh weaker than Rowan's. But he wonders if thinking that is itself a form of self-aggrandisement. If he falls, he will go down, right down, leaving his smashed body on the ground, and descend to Hell, the fiery torment, and there will be no escaping it, having died unshriven, steeped in the sin of Pride.

But something is happening — Kenneth's hand is in his own; he is pulling, hauling him towards the sky. With a great heave, a final effort, he finds himself at the cliff top. Ahead of him is the joined loch, a vast expanse of water. And on a small island there is a tall building with towers and turrets, but no walls, connected to the shore by a narrow causeway. It is exactly as Gervaise described it. In the dense mist, it seems dreamily insubstantial, as if resting on cloud.

'The Abbey of Saint Medard,' says Kenneth. 'God has been our guide.'

XVI

He leaves, in great commotion; the cavalcade crashes across the drawbridge. Wulva watches till he is out of sight. They did not speak after the first hunt, nor was she asked to hunt with him again. She is relieved but feels empty. There seems no purpose to things; her head is reeling. She doesn't fear the witches' wrath; she is too numb to fear them. She tries to soothe her spirit with her daily round, but her talk is stilted, and she can't bring her full attention to any task. Is this madness? Or its starting place? Has he ensnared her, somehow, without so much as giving her one kiss? Working at her embroidery — a woodland scene of flowers and branches, deer and hare — she pricks herself and the blood falls on the sampler. She lets it dry, as she let the boar's blood dry on her face, at his command. Macbeth. The others are just phantoms. He is a man.

A week or so later, a messenger arrives. She hears a commotion in the solar, Macduff and Aefric shouting. They are quarrelling again! She has hardly ever heard them raise their voices to each other. There are running feet, and a maidservant comes to fetch her.

'My lady has some news!' The maid's expression is that of an eavesdropper who has heard more than they bargained for. 'God love you, and give you grace!'

'It is quite shocking,' says Aefric, in greeting. 'There was nothing to suggest it.'

'Suggest what?'

Macduff has his back turned and is looking out of the window. 'It makes perfect sense. He bided his time.'

'Not much time!' cries Aefric, angrily. She wipes her eyes.

'Gave himself a period of reflection, to decide upon it.'

Wulva frowns. 'Decide upon what, sir?'

'My lord Macbeth wishes to marry you,' says Macduff, turning to face her. 'I hope that is agreeable to you.'

'Marry?' She looks at Aefric. 'I thought he hated me.'

'Whatever made you think that?' says Aefric. 'And what a thing to say! No doubt his feelings were confused, at first, it being so soon after his lady's untimely end … But now, he is determined on it. My lord Macduff will accompany you. North. To Moray. And the marriage will take place there.'

She is too shocked to speak at first, then blurts out: 'No hand-fasting here, beforehand? Isn't that the custom?'

'Not always.' Aefric doesn't meet her eye. But Wulva is glad of this. They both know how much is missing of what normally would pass between them — advice and love and wisdom. In this matter, Aefric does not have the power to help her. Wulva trembles, but her goal is fixed. She will do as she is bidden.

When she is alone, she is filled with horror and triumph. A great joy is welling up inside her, and she knows there's something evil in it. She fears her own craving, now soon to be sated. She fears the man.

Journey, reunion, wedding. It is a dream, a weird hallucination. There is talk, there are people; she speaks, she eats, she listens. But there is nothing real but him. Dressed in silk and velvet, her skin burns at every touch. After the oath, she goes up first, alone, to a tower room, its walls so steep they form the roof. Removes the shimmering, encasing gown, lies naked in the cold wide bed. When he appears, she pushes the covers back so he can see her. He kneels by the door. Unclothed, the mormaer is thin, white-fleshed, his muscles hard and small. Black hair sprouts from his back, along his limbs. His belly's flat, his prick is long. He's peeled and awkward, trembling. She slithers over the rushes and slips herself around him. Berthe's breasts are milk-suck. Merrow's cunt is fish-stink. Cailleach weaves the spell.

His castle stands on a mountain top, its high walls surmounting jagged cliffs. Inside, there are bones and skins, and hunting dogs the size of ponies. Antlers are mounted on the walls, and white skulls with black eye-sockets. Furs and pelts fill the solar, hanging on every wall. There are wolf-hides everywhere, souls trapped in the snarling heads. Wulva strokes the long, coarse guard hairs, and pushes her fingers down into the soft undercoat. Her own hide prickles.

They are married, joined, made one. She feels his presence no matter where he is. If he looks at her, she feels joy in possession; if he looks away, she's null and empty. His attention is his power, given and withheld without explanation. She cannot bear to see him restless. Most of his conversation is with his soldiers and attendants. There is much to plan, it seems, much to decide and organise, to seek and plunder. When he is caught up in a scheme, his eyes are bright, and he draws lines upon the table with his knife — these men *here*, those men *there*, this is their weakness, this is our strength. The days are measured out in tasks, in feasts, in circling conversations.

It is right that she should play the wife. She wears her gowns, she combs her hair, she braves the heat in the seething kitchens, giving her opinion about the pies and offal, wine and small-beer, eel and venison. It seems as if there is feasting every day. Thanes and their men arrive, to eat and drink and share their thoughts and grievances. No one is satisfied, everyone has a tale to tell; the mountains are steeped in memories of wrong.

Their business is done mostly at night-time. Their

shivering communions stir her horribly. When they are seared together, he forgets she's not his equal. She sees the yearning in him. He has her, but must have more, beyond the bed, beyond the castle. He is not content with being the mormaer of this distant place, a slab of mountain and surrounding land, with the blood-feuds of his rivals. He craves more, in the bitter dark, and he tells her of it.

One night, she gets up and goes to the open window, through which the cold wind blows, chilling her naked flesh. Far off, beyond the loch, deep in the forest, she hears howling, the call of those she lost. Then she turns, and sees that he is watching her from the bed. His eyes are yellow and inhuman. When she returns to him, she finds him different, bestial — she's terrified, whinnying and snorting. In the morning, his hairy lips kiss her tenderly.

XVII

They cross the causeway, which is several feet above the loch. Rowan sees how the surface of the water is pitted by falling raindrops. There is a stout door inside the gatehouse, fretted with iron-work. When they turn the handle, the door creaks open to reveal a vast quadrangle. The cobbles are overgrown with weeds and grasses, and three ravens look down, perched on a weathervane. Blind windows stare out from the surrounding walls, and a stone stairway leads up to the encircling walkway. Kenneth pauses momentarily and looks around, before marching up the steps, with Rowan close behind, heart beating fast, his mind filled with a mixture of fear and wonder. They enter the cloister, where the fountain splashes gently in the midst of towering weeds. The benches set into the enclosing walls are green with slime, and a great toad flops across the passageway in front of them. It is a particularly ugly creature, its skin wrinkled and wart-blistered. The flumping of its body across the stone flags is the only sound in the silent cloister. The silence is unsettling. Kenneth stops to examine the whetstone, as if it might give up some secret.

The two men pass storerooms and the calefactory — which has a fireplace so enormous a man might take up residence inside it — and then enter the refectory. Here the long dining tables remain, with stools ranged in front of them, and there is a Bible attached to the stone pulpit, though its pages are stained and wrinkled. Rowan fears that this does not bode well for the condition of the books in the library. There is a pungent smell of damp, and puddles of water in the chapter house. In the kitchen, they find a room with the capacity to feed an army, with three fireplaces down one side. Although there is little sign of man-made damage, it seems that someone has been here already: all that remains is some furniture. When they reach the abbey church, they see that it has been badly damaged by fire, although the other buildings they have seen are untouched. The shell of the building has survived, but the frescos are blurred and blackened, and most of the windows are shattered, with just a few panes of coloured glass remaining. Miraculously, in the south transept, the tall narrow window behind the altar has been preserved, and the crucified Christ looks down at them, mournful and forgiving. Above the window, set in an alcove, there is a white marble statue of the risen Christ, holding out his arms in beatific welcome. Kenneth kneels on the damp stone and crosses himself. Rowan does likewise, and bows his head. However, this discovery has not comforted him. If anything, his sense of foreboding has increased.

They continue their search of the monastery, and proceed to the abbey house. The rooms on the upper floor are empty, save for a few items of furniture, and the glass in the windows is intact. In the centre of the house there is a quadrangle garden, with three yew trees, around which plants and flowers have flourished in lush profusion. It does not look natural — it seems another miracle — that this garden should be so abundant, on this mountain, in this blighted house of God. Rowan almost cries out when he sees it. It is not divided into segments and organised accordingly but seems haphazard, its trees, shrubs, vines, and flowers all entangled, as if the gardener had made it blindly. There are tansies, marigolds, gillyflowers, and periwinkles, while violets, daisies, and primroses peer up from the tall grass. Medicinal flowers and ornamental blooms grow cheek by jowl, like squires and peasants in a May Day crowd. Its scent is a mix of lilies and roses with fragrant herbs — basil, rosemary, and lavender. The rose bushes are of enormous size, as big as young oaks, and their blooms are the size of cabbages. Which cannot be so, and he must doubt the evidence of his own eyes. The rigours of his journey have got the better of him. He looks for a way down to the garden but can see no way to enter it. Kenneth, coming up behind him, stares blankly. He is shaking slightly. Rowan notices how pale he looks; his skin is clammy, and his eyes are dull.

'Are you quite well, brother?' asks Rowan.

'This abbey gives me the ague.'

'Look at this astonishing garden,' says Rowan. 'It seems God-given. Another miracle, like the altar!'

'Something terrible has happened here,' says Kenneth. There is a catch in his voice that takes Rowan by surprise.

'Indeed, yes, the monks were wiped out by the pestilence.'

'But where is the evidence of this? Where are the graves?'

'Perhaps the bodies were removed. Others have been here before us.'

Kenneth bites his lip. 'I don't like it. Pray God protect us.'

Rowan looks back at the garden. He realises that the trees are filled with birds, and he listens for a while to the fluid song of a blackbird.

'Does anything about this garden strike you as remarkable?' asks Rowan.

'An inconvenient location. And no sign of an entrance. But I have never had much interest in gardens. The garden is the least of our concerns, brother.'

Rowan's gaze returns to the garden, this time noting the luxuriant fruit trees bearing apple, pear, and quince, walnuts, filberts, and fat plums. Has he ever seen such a garden? Has he ever seen such natural riches, such peerless splendour? The grapes on the vines are deepest purple, drooping heavily from the straining branches. Kenneth is right: there is something strange about the place. Perhaps the Devil has indeed played a part in its construction.

Kenneth turns away. 'I will leave you to your

explorations. With luck, you will find the library. This place is the endpoint of our quest. Now it is for you to accomplish the task you have been given. I intend to spend my time in prayer and fasting.'

Rowan watches him go, noting that he is walking a little unsteadily. This quest has taken its toll on both of them. He sends up another prayer to God.

By the end of the day, Rowan has made a thorough search of the monastery, keeping careful notes and recording his progress as accurately as he can, writing on a fragment of his precious parchment. His notes and diagrams indicate no over-arching plan, and he feels as if he is charting his journey around some natural formation, rather than one born of human thought and design. There's a confusing number of passageways, colonnades, cloisters, stairways. When he is walking from one building to another, he sometimes feels a sense that he is repeating the same action, and is entering for the second time. Even the views out of the windows confuse him: he cannot get his bearings as to its geographical situation. The constant rain does not help: its sound permeates every part of the empty monastery.

When he climbs the bell tower and looks out at the joined lochs, he is perturbed to see the wildness of the water, which has the appearance of a storm-wracked ocean. In one of the passages, he is lost in the contemplation of a fresco that seems as real to him as the monastery itself, ornate and untranslatable, showing figures unfamiliar from scripture. Queer things to find in a religious house, depicted with such skill that they seem brighter and more alive than he feels himself. They remind him, uncomfortably, of the occult signs and patterns on the tapestries he saw in that accursed house in Edinburgh. At the very end of the day, as the light is fading, he finds a scriptorium. Here there is a Christian fresco, he is relieved to see, showing scenes from the life of Jacob the patriarch: covered in hairy goatskin so that he may take the birthright of his hirsute brother; making love to Leah and Rachel; wrestling with an angel; and, finally, confronted by a ladder, with angels ascending and descending.

At the centre of the room there is a large rectangular table, wide enough to lie on and ten feet long. The shelves beneath are empty, and the wall benches have been tipped over. A tall window — with plain, mullioned glass — gives good light, despite the lateness of the hour. He feels a kinship with the monks who once toiled here, writing till their eyes blurred and then resting on those benches, with a modicum of fine-wrought work to show for it at the end of each long day. He walks the length of the table, running his finger through the dust on its surface. Bending down to look beneath, he sees that one of the shelves is not empty after all — there is a single volume lying there. He picks it up and opens it. To his surprise, he finds that it is not a conventional book, with parchment bound between calfskin covers, but a form of box. It contains a single key: a shining copper key. Could this have belonged to the amarius, who had charge of both scriptorium and library? He looks around; the only door that he can see in the room is the one through which he entered. The key doesn't fit its lock. He looks at it, wondering. Few of the doors he has passed through have been closed, as those who came before and plundered the building have forced them open. Some have been smashed to pieces. So it is possible that this key will fit one such door, and has no significance, no further use. But he turns it over in his hand. Why was it hidden in a book? His curiosity is piqued. He will explore further tomorrow, in the light of morning.

Rowan retraces his steps carefully at the end of the day, for it seems possible at any moment that he might take a wrong turn and lose himself. His head is aching and he has a growing sense of unease. The not-rightness of the monastery is making him disoriented, and he shares Kenneth's sense that the place is in some way malign. In his bones, his gut, he feels that there is something ill-omened about it. He finds Kenneth in the chapel, prostrate before the preserved altar. The statue of the risen Christ seems to give off its own light, but the rest of the ruined chapel is filled with shadow. For some time, he waits for Kenneth to finish his prayers, but after ten minutes or so, he calls out softly to him.

Kenneth looks up, and gets slowly to his feet. Rowan

sees that he is wearing vestments. When he draws closer, their damp stench is unmistakeable.

'Wherever did you get those?'

'From a chest in one of the solars.'

'But mightn't they be infected?'

'The pestilence is long gone.'

Kenneth has no proof of this, but Rowan doesn't have the stomach to disagree.

'How long have you been here?'

Kenneth shrugs. 'I couldn't say.'

'Really, you will make yourself ill. You must come with me and eat, then take some rest.'

Kenneth comes with him, and they enter a solar in the chapter house. Rowan sees that Kenneth has left their packs there. He lights a candle and finds some bread and cheese.

But Kenneth does not touch his food. 'This is a cursed place,' he says. 'The Devil walks here.' He is sitting cross-legged, like a schoolboy.

'You have said so already. I share your disquiet, brother, and will finish here as quickly as I can. But I have yet to find the library, unfortunately.'

Kenneth stares at him. 'May God protect and save us,' he says.

'Such piety does you credit, but perhaps you should rest now. That chapel certainly has a curious atmosphere. I would not like to spend long alone there myself.'

'I am a fighting man, Brother Rowan; that is my natural

home. I know where I am when I am among other men, with a clear task and a quiver of new arrows.'

Rowan breaks off a corner of bread and begins to eat. It is dry and tasteless. 'Yet you have taken to the life of the cloister very well.'

'No. I see now that the walls were doing me a service. The enclosure shut me into certain routines of worship. But I have not adapted to it, and I cannot adapt to it; I came to it too late. And —' He stops and bows his head. 'I have prayed and prayed, and asked the Maker to have mercy. But there is something here.'

Rowan has broken off some more bread. 'What, brother? What is here?'

Kenneth looks at the opposite wall, as if he's seeing pictures. 'It was an honour to go on Crusade to Spain. It was an honour to lay waste to the Infidel. Through that labour, I was in the service of Our Lord. We prayed before entering battle.'

'Yes, of course. You acquitted yourself heroically.'

'I have no idea how many I dispatched. It was all confusion, as all battles are, once they begin. The planning may be ordered, but the execution is muddled with stinking gore.' Kenneth shifts and re-crosses his legs.

'I understand what you are saying.'

'No man can fully understand if he has not served in battle himself. A soldier does what he is told to do. There is no use dwelling on the nature of the deaths you must administer —' His voice catches, and he lowers his head again. 'There was one boy, however ... I stumbled upon him when we had let our arrows fly and were advancing towards the enemy. He'd fallen, and his comrades had left him to die. I doubt if he was twelve.'

'You must pray for his immortal soul.'

'An Infidel, though! A Godless heathen, bound for the Eternal Fire? My prayers will never reach him. He was screaming, though half his face was meat. Horrible, most horrible. Twitching and making such a sound — not human, not manly. I suppose he would have had more courage had he been English.'

'Let this alone, brother. These thoughts are coming to you because your mind's afflicted.'

'So I killed him. Cut his head off, in one fell swoop, whoosh! It left his body, jumped off his neck.' He stares at the wall again. 'It was the strangest thing. So vile, yet almost ordinary. Just common butchery, our daily bread.'

'Put this from you; it does no good.'

'I have not thought of it, till now. This other horror, which will not leave me. Yet, as in battle, I was acting for the Maker! Destroying what had been wrought by the Devil. During my prayers, I realised that I could hear something, which at first I took for rats.'

'What was this sound?'

'Something scuttling and snorting.'

'A spirit, you mean? The walking dead?'

'Worse even than that, I fear, for I know that sound from the evil house in Edinburgh.'

'Are you speaking of that half-breed creature?'

'That devilish being, yes. Made with the lore of Lucifer. And then — poof! It goes away.'

'You are over-wrought. I assure you, this place is empty. I have heard nothing but the endless rain. Go and rest awhile.'

'But supposing ...' Kenneth seems to search for the right words. 'Supposing a thing, not properly alive, not the work of the Maker, might not die? As it could never fully live, suppose that instead of dying, it inhabits a sort of hinterland?'

'Such as purgatory?'

'No, that's for Christian souls. Supposing it remains earth-bound, undead? I felt something plucking at my sleeve: a cursed, pig-man's hand.'

'This is foolish talk. What you describe is just the memory of nightmare.'

'I felt it. He put a curse on me, that demon-scholar. I should have slain him too. I have said my prayers, I have begged forgiveness, but the air was empty! God was elsewhere.'

Blood begets blood, thinks Rowan. The soldier's logic. He finishes his meal and arranges his makeshift bed. Kenneth sits motionless. After he has said Vespers, Rowan sees that Kenneth has taken out his knife and is examining the blade, as if something stains it.

XVIII

He's off, then, to war. Looks up as he passes beneath her window but makes no sign. Soon after, she feels a change, as if the curse is coming. A taste of metal in her mouth. She craves sweet possets, then rabbit liver, then nothing but fried pig's ears. There is no doubt what this signifies, but she's unwilling at first to admit it. Having a child will transform her; the darkness of their union will be made flesh. She is not ready. It is too soon. But the sickness worsens, and she throws up every meal.

'He will be pleased,' say her serving women knowingly. 'This is a great gift to give the master, on his return.'

And when he does come back, he's joyful. His eyes stay on her. It will be a boy, he knows it. The cocoon holds them as the months go by. When they are alone, he sings to the distended dome that holds the baby. When they are in company, he says she is 'his queen'. Looks are exchanged — the queen of what, exactly? But she is ill, and each day she feels worse. Her cravings become strange: for swan's eggs, stag brain, calf-lips. Meat and meat and more meat; she cannot stomach fruit or greens. Her belly grows, her body shrinks, she is not sufficient to be host of what she carries. Her whole self seems to be contained within this tight-stretched sac. Some nights her fancy is that she is to give birth to herself, that she is snared inside her own belly, drowning in her own waters, and the only way out of her prison is through her hole.

And so Macbeth becomes her gaoler, and she his possession. The mindless lust that made a willing beast of her subsides, and she sees them as they are: separate, man and woman, bound by seed, and promise, and his will. As the baby grows inside her, so she must shrink, her purpose being to birth it. She spends her days in the solar, toppling, swollen, hideous to her own eyes, but not to his. She must always be taking off her nightgown so he can see this great thing she has become. There seems to be little space in her head for any thoughts to fit, her head being no bigger than a pea, attached to a great whale. But what does come to her, time and again, unbidden, is a dread of what she'll bring forth. The size is wrong; it is so big. And that's not all: the way she is seems strange. This is not how it was with Aefric, nor the other women she helped give birth when she lived at Macduff's castle. Nothing she can do about it, trapped in her fat self, dumb and meat-fed. The more Macbeth rejoices in her, the more she fears what's to come. He wishes to fornicate every night, lying beneath her great belly, but she persuades him that it's unsafe, and sleeps alone. And when she is alone, her minds loops and turns in dread.

She has good reason to be fearful. Waiting for the birth of his son does not improve Macbeth's temper. A servant boy spills the wine, and is hanged in the courtyard for all to see. A chase hound snaps at him, and he slashes its throat and throws it to the other dogs for dinner. When he's not enraged, he clings to her, insatiable: she must sit upon his knee; he must feel her belly; they must talk of the heroic qualities his new son will display. As if she were herself a child, he insists on feeding her by hand, spiking chunks of meat with his dagger and sliding the blade between her lips.

There is madness in the air, she feels it like a pall. Her chance comes when Macbeth leaves to fight another battle. As soon as he is out of sight, she rides out of the castle. By some instinct, she knows which way to go, and crosses barren moorland, through a forest of ancient pine, and then comes to a wide beach. The sky is pale, and bleached sand stretches to the horizon, a wasteland between land and sea. Kicking the palfrey on, she canters across the sand, making for the distant sea-line. Seabirds dive and glide above her head. When she reaches the ocean, the waves surge around her, and her skirts are drenched and heavy. A sea-mist comes down, blotting out the sun. The air is thickening and shifting around her, a cloud of dark unknowing. Then she makes out, dimly at first, three figures, carrying a rounded boat. They come slowly towards her and set it down.

She calls out: 'You made me marry a monster. And now I'm having his child. Why have you done this?'

Cailleach comes forward and takes the horse's bridle. 'But you like him, don't you?' she says, leering. 'You're doing your task with all the guile of Satan and his crew.'

'*Like?* That is not the word. You have bewitched me, and I have bewitched him. And now there's something wrong. I can't stay until the child is born. I dread the day it comes. This man is cruel. You speak of Satan, but he is like the Devil.'

'Which suits our purpose.'

'Yours, not mine! I don't belong here.'

'You don't belong anywhere. That's why we marked you.'

Wulva sees that the fog has rolled away and all is bright and shining, extending to the edge of sight. The light is dazzling; the witches loom like visions. One maid, one matron, one crone.

'The Mormaer of Moray has married you, and shown you his base nature. That is well done,' says aged Cailleach. 'You are carrying his child, so be it; you are young and fertile, so no surprise. But this is only the beginning. You must accomplish more.'

'I have no power; I'm his chattel! That is where you planted me.'

'You have his ear,' says milk-fat Berthe. 'At dead of night.' She mimics fornication.

'You haunt his dreams,' says maiden Merrow, translucent against the sea.

Cailleach draws a large circle in the sand. When it's done, she pours a vial of liquid into the centre, which melts and burns the grains. Beetles and crabs scuttle away. The circle spreads and creeps, like a bloodstain after slaughter, so that after a few moments the whole circle is a gleaming mirror. Yet it does not reflect the sky above but seems to contain some queerness of its own — darkness and shifting shards of light.

'Let us all be seated, around this circle,' says Cailleach. 'And we shall see what's yet to come.'

Wulva takes her place, arranging her wet skirts about her. Bright wind is tearing off the sea, spattering her with salt water. Cailleach is silent. She pulls herself tighter, so that she shrinks to half her size, then breathes out and grows as big as a grounded walrus. Everything around her starts to lose its colour, and the sound of the waves dulls and weakens. The circle seems to grow, so that all Wulva can see is the interplay of light and shadow. Cailleach raises her head, and seems to listen. Then she nods, and begins: 'Scale of dragon, tooth of wolf, Witches' mummy; maw and gulf, Root of hemlock, digged in dark, Gall of goat and slips of yew ...' The mirror morphs and broils; images come and go like night-fears. 'Adder's fork and blind-worm's sting, Lizard's leg and howlet's wing, For a charm of powerful trouble, Like a hell-broth, boil and bubble.' The mirror clears, like a day dawning, then darkens again. A picture begins to emerge. Wulva strains to see.

It is the mormaer's castle, perfect in every detail. She can see each separate trunk of the oak palisade, the courtyard, where a groom is saddling up a destrier, and there — she almost cries out — the figure of the mormaer himself, coming down the steps from the keep. He approaches the groom and speaks to him, though there is no discernible sound. It is as if she is present, spying on her husband, but from a great distance.

'When is this? Is it happening at this moment?' she asks, but Cailleach only raises a finger to her lips, requesting silence.

Others are assembling, and their horses are brought out from the stables. They mount and ride out of the castle, crossing the drawbridge and cantering along the road towards the mountains. The mirror darkens again, and this time she sees a battlefield, in a place she doesn't recognise. The scene is one of violence and bloodshed, man and horse alike maimed and bloody, the ground strewn with the dead and dying — swords hacking, stabbing, a soundless panorama of the damned. There is the mormaer, still on horseback, plunging a spear into the neck of a man lying on the ground in front of him. The view shifts with a jerk, so that she sees only the mormaer's face, and his expression of triumphant glee. There is blood on his forehead, and his eyes are shining with excitement. The vision fades in a surge of crimson.

'That is the man, is it not?' says Cailleach. 'Your man?'

Wulva nods. 'Why must I see this? I know what he is already.'

'He must destroy the enemy, lest they do the same to him.'

'Yes, the mormaer system.'

Cailleach waves her hand, and the scene changes. An old man on a stone throne, a gold crown on his head. Men and women wait to speak to him, and to this one he speaks quietly, to that one he gives money. The vision shifts, seems to fly over the city — she sees scaffolding, workmen, ladders. Now it passes over the city walls, and reaches a mighty forest. But there is no peace there: birds fly helter-skelter above the trees, cawing and shrieking; the forest creatures flee; the men have axes, ropes, and carts. They cut down the trees and make great fires of them. The fires spread, smouldering at first, glowing red and orange, then torching a single tree, running up the trunk, flaring skywards. The forest is becoming an inferno. Higher and higher the flames mount, and run beyond the woodland, eating heathlands, scrub, heather, leaping streams and rivers, consuming everything. As the fire rages, so the seas rise up, over the sand, over the shingle, beyond, flooding the land, making an ocean of it. Icebergs crack and break apart, and the skies are torn by a silent storm. The sea itself is flaming. Whales lie dead on scarlet beaches, the sky burns bright with colours she has never seen. A great cloud, shaped like a fungus, in the distance, then everything burns white.

'I don't know what this means,' she says. 'Why must I see this? Is it purgatory or Hell?'

'They have the power,' says Berthe. 'The mormaers. That is what we've shown you.'

'And we have none,' says Merrow.

'What's this to do with me? They will destroy what they choose. I can't stop them.'

'It is true that we are weak, according to their logic, and they are strong, by their estimation. So we must be clever,' says Cailleach. 'If we use our skill, we can make their own power work against them.'

'How is that possible?'

'If we can't destroy them, then they must destroy themselves. We can see that they are willing students, and they have an aptitude for self-destruction. The sooner they succeed in ending their own kind, the sooner the rest of us will begin to mend. The natural order will be restored.'

'But who are "they"? The mormaers are not monsters! Is every person doomed?'

'There is space for humans on the Earth, but not for this breed, so violent and greedy. Remember what I taught you, those words in the holy book. They think they have dominion. And they put no limit on their ambition. Their appetites are remorseless; once they have something, they must have more. They eat until they fatten, they drink until they fall down drunk, they fornicate until the land fills with their spawn. This has already started. They'll kill every wolf in Scotland before they're done.'

A cloud passes over the mirror, then she sees Macbeth's face again. 'This man will be king, with your assistance,' says Cailleach.

'How can that help? Why do you want this?'

'He will set in motion the pattern of destruction that we desire. The more of his kind rule, the quicker they will wreak their own destruction. Blood begets blood — that is their logic. The present king is kindly. Such men drag us down, with their soft looks and seeming benevolence. They'll see us out, species by species, tribe by tribe, speaking of trade routes and safe passages. But the bloody man is our man, he and his kin, with his ceaseless wars.'

'I've been treated with love and kindness, and I've seen their cruelty too.' She feels faint, and puts her hands upon her belly. 'What of my child?'

'Help us destroy the mormaers and their plans, and all of us will prosper,' says Cailleach. 'You will be free. So urge them on, to their destruction. Make Macbeth king, and his lands will run with blood.'

'You speak in riddles. How should I do that?'

The three witches exchange glances. 'King Duncan will come to visit,' says Merrow.

'And he is pleased with your mormaer,' says Bertha. 'He has killed well.'

'We will meet him on the road. When he returns to you, we will have planted the seeds that you must water. Do you understand? You must use your ... what would you say ...'

'Your charms,' says Berthe, with a ragged smile.

'He craves that crown, though he's yet to realise it. His spirit's vaporous. He's corruptible. Feed his dreaming with your woman's bile, make him see this blood-crown is his for the taking,' says Cailleach. 'Help us put it on his head.'

XIX

Rowan takes the key and resumes his search, leaving Kenneth praying and chanting in the great chapel. Kenneth insists on wearing the damp vestments again, despite Rowan's protestations. His lone voice rises up in the vast space:

> *O come let us sing unto the Lord:*
> *Let us make a joyful noise to the rock of our salvation,*
> *Let us come before his presence with our thanksgiving,*
> *And make a joyful noise unto him with psalms.*

Yet the noise is not joyful. Perhaps it was when there were many voices joined in daily worship, but not now. Kenneth's prayer seems to make the abbey emptier and more forbidding. Its echo follows Rowan as he proceeds back to the library, carried along the deserted corridors and cloisters.

*For the Lord is a great God, and great King
above all gods.
In his hand are the deep places of the earth:
The strength of the hills is his also.
The sea is his, and he made it, and his hands
formed the dry land,
O come let us worship and bow down:
Let us kneel before the Lord our maker.*

He has slept well enough but was aware of the sound of rainfall during the night. This morning, there is a palpable sense of damp in the chapter house, and he is obliged to run between the monastery buildings, bent double, in the downpour. It gives him a sense of foreboding, and he wonders if the monastery is safe from flood. Could the waters of the loch rise higher? He climbs the bell tower, and goes onto the roof, blinking raindrops out of his eyes. The wind-tossed waters of the loch certainly seem higher, and down below he can see the water lapping at the walls.

Back in the scriptorium, Rowan investigates the shelves beneath the writing table, where yesterday he found the hollow book. He feels sure that this hiding place has some significance. But he finds nothing, apart from the clenched body of a dead house-spider. Then he thinks to look again at the book that held the key, which is still lying on the table. He looks at the space which the key occupied, cut into the wooden interior, and then teases at the edge of the wooden block until it loosens. He lifts it out. Underneath, there is a tiny drawing of the scriptorium, perfectly detailed and accurate, so delicately done that surely a fairy hand has made it. It is an exact copy of the room he sees in front of him, if he stands facing the window, except that there are papers and documents stacked on the shelves, and two monks sitting copying at the table. Then he notices something else. Behind them is a stepladder, with seven rungs, positioned exactly halfway along the left-hand wall. He looks up — there is no ladder there now. But when he searches the room, he finds one inside a tall cupboard; it too has seven rungs. Rowan props the ladder against the left-hand wall and climbs up, moving stiffly. When he reaches the top, he looks around, narrowing his eyes. He can see nothing of note, just gilded panelling. Another thought strikes him, and he descends the ladder, and then moves it a foot to the right. He climbs it, looks upward and around, and then descends and moves it once again, and again, eventually circumnavigating the room. When he has reached the place where he started, he sighs. Perhaps the drawing means nothing. But then he looks again at the great fresco that covers one wall, and his attention is caught by Jacob's ladder, set on the Earth but reaching up to Heaven, with the angels ascending and descending. He props the ladder against the fresco. Climbing up, he examines the painting more closely and sees that the space between the sixth and seventh rungs is slightly raised from the rest of the fresco, that it is, in fact, a panel. He feels along its edge and finds a catch, and, to his delight, the panel springs open.

Hardly daring to breathe, he puts in his hand, fearing to be bitten by a rat as he feels around inside, but finds only dust. Then he runs his hand across the higher part of the interior, the area above the hidden door. His fingers find a small handle, which he pulls. Below him, to the left side of the propped ladder, and at the foot of the great ladder in the fresco, the panelling swings open to reveal a door. It is three feet high or thereabouts, and scarcely two feet wide. Eureka! He descends the ladder, takes the key from his pocket, and tries it in the lock. The lock is rusty, and it sticks at first, but after a few seconds of jiggling, he feels it turn, and the door opens. Giving thanks for his slight build, he lights a candle and squeezes through. He looks around: this is what he has been seeking. A hidden library. It is long and narrow, with lecterns ranged along the walls. The shelves underneath the lecterns are stacked with books, pancartes, and parchment rolls, and each book is attached to the lectern with a chain.

Rowan sniffs the air — the library has not escaped the seeping damp that has affected the rest of the monastery. Even here, on the second floor, the waters have done their work. Many of the parchments, unprotected by leather bindings, are in a ruinous state, and all he can make out is a word here and there. Mostly they are blurred and pitted, damaged beyond redemption. If anything of value was written there, he is not going to find it. But it may be that the books are in better order, having been afforded the protection of their bindings. He places his lantern in an alcove above one of the lecterns and heaves a volume onto the top. Opening it, he sees that the contents are indeed better preserved. The title is *The Book of Life's Merits*, and the author Hildegard of Bingen. He quickly establishes that the work is a description of the physical reality of purgatory, its situation not being some other-worldly place between Heaven and Hell, but a geographical location on the surface of the solid, temporal world. In other circumstances, Rowan might have spent many happy hours perusing this volume. The descriptions of sin are certainly arresting, and the book may have much to teach him. But it is not what he is seeking, and he can't afford to wander along paths of uncertain relevance and passing interest, as men are wont to do in libraries. He sighs and rubs his eyes, refocuses his attention. The smell of damp is stronger here than in the outer room, and he can hear the sound of trickling water. He notices that the chains that bind the volumes to the lecterns are rusted. Attention, attention. He is searching for the Scottish king-line. Where shall he find it? There is no sign of water damage to this book, but he wonders if the volumes lower down the piles might have been more seriously affected. A brief investigation shows that this is the case: Rowan estimates that there are around fifty books in the cell-like library and a similar number of bundles of parchment. It's a relief that there are shelf lists pasted to the walls above each lectern, which itemise the works stored below. These must have stayed above the level of the floodwater, as they are still legible. He reads these — slow work, with only the flickering candlelight to aid him — and finds that there is little among the bound works that is germane to his research. The collection is eclectic and extraordinary: *Lights Lofty of Form to Reveal the Secrets of the Pyramids* and *The Incoherence of the Incoherence*. What does cheer him is that some of the documents are not chained to the lecterns.

He takes these outside, into the scriptorium, and studies them carefully. A significant number are unreadable, but one of them contains the names of certain kings: Alpín mac Echdach, alleged king of Dal Riata; Coinneach mac Ailpein, first king of Alba; Domhnall mac Solein, once king of the Picts; Còiseam mac Choinnich, and several others. These names appear on different pages, lost among other names and references that he doesn't recognise. The most recent is Lughlagh mac Gille Chomghain. Is the record continual or broken? He can't tell; the pages are too badly damaged. Ever meticulous, he returns the rest of the material to the library, and closes the door.

Going back to the pile of damaged documents, he takes out his own parchment roll, spreads it out on one of the lecterns, prepares his writing tools and begins, painstakingly, to make a copy of those names that might be pertinent. He works slowly, frowning, and listening to the rain. It seems to be gaining in intensity, and the wind moans and rattles against the long window next to the image of Jacob and the ladder. Rowan looks out. There are black clouds in the sky, and the loch is churning violently. The sooner he completes the work, the sooner they can leave.

Taking up his quill, he dips it in the oak-gall and begins to write, studying the text. The ancient names bring images of wild mountains and warriors raging across the heath. He stares tiredly at the scuffed signs that convey the messages, and makes his own, new and clear, outlines on his parchment, then falls into a sort of trance, in which these warriors from long ago are more real to him than his own body. Then he feels a hand on his shoulder, and cries out in alarm. He looks up. Kenneth, in his vestments, pale and cadaverous.

'Brother! You startled me!'

'When will this be finished?' asks Kenneth. His voice is quivering with emotion.

'I'm working as quickly as I can, but I must be thorough, and you can see the state of the documents. They are in a similar condition to that cassock. I wish you would put it away. Wearing a dead man's vestments is rather morbid.'

'If they are unfinished, then take them with you! We cannot tarry here.'

'That's impossible, I regret to say. They scarcely survived being moved from the library to this lectern. There is no way I could remove them, even if that were ethical.'

Kenneth closes his eyes and raises his hands. 'By Heaven!

Do you think that has bothered anyone else who's come here? Why do you think this place is in the state it's in?'

'Brother, may I remind you that I am a scholar and a man of God, not a looter? I am surprised to hear you say such a thing. You are distressed, I can see that, but I must do what I have come to do, and I must do it in the proper fashion. As soon as I have done so, we can go.'

Kenneth's strange demeanour seems to have some contagion in it, and he senses the echoing abbey that encloses them: the vast and empty rooms, the spaces in between, the shadowed courtyards, the voided cloisters, the remorseless waters lapping against the stone.

'This place is cursed,' says Kenneth. 'I don't know what went on here, but it was evil. Something wrong has happened, and it will destroy us if we don't depart forthwith.'

'Come now, that is utter nonsense. It is an abandoned abbey, empty since the pestilence. There is no mystery in it. If ever a place were to have a forbidding atmosphere, it would be this one. I am sorry that you are upset, but it has as much to do with your history as it does with our being here. Have your prayers brought you no peace?'

'Peace? How shall I come by peace? I might pray till I am older than Methuselah, and it would make no difference. God's nails! Lucifer is stalking this place. Those noises, scuffling, shuffling, follow everywhere I go. I tell you, it's a cursed and appalling ruin. They have driven out the Maker and put the Devil in his stead.'

'Oh Kenneth, this is your fancy, your imagination playing tricks …'

'Don't speak of things of which you know nothing. When I prayed, in that great chapel, that once-chapel, now corrupted, there was an echo, which hurled the words and songs of worship back at me.'

'Listen, please, can we have a rational conversation …'

'Hurled them back, mis-ordered them, and made them diabolic! God has fled this place, and Satan's here, I tell you.'

'Really, I never heard such madness.'

'Lucifer is as real as God Almighty, and he preys on the unwary. You know that, brother, you know that he can take on any form, deceive us, make fools of us. There was a route to Heaven in this place once, and now the fissure's opened up to Hell. God's blood, will you not listen to me?'

Rowan has his own sense of unease about the place, but he knows that good Christians are protected by their faith. Those who wander from the true path, into heresy and superstition, are at most risk from the Devil. 'If you are so anxious about the Evil One, might I suggest that you desist from taking Our Lord's name in vain? Let us remember that we are men of God, and that we must conduct ourselves accordingly.' Rowan sets down his quill, and tightens the top of his inkwell. 'Let us go and pray, and then have something to eat. Let us restore some order, and regain a sense of proportion in this matter.'

'I have prayed and prayed — did you not hear me say so?

God can't hear us in this benighted ruin! And I am fasting, and shall not pollute my body with food until my soul is free of torment. But the truth is that I can't reach God, and the reason I can't reach Him is that He has left us.'

'God cannot leave! He is omnipresent and omniscient. God is always with us. You forget Christ's promise, the New Testament, by which we live. You are losing your wits.'

'Supposing that's not true?' says Kenneth in a whisper. 'I saw it in the eyes of that Gervaise. He is an unbeliever. He's set himself up to rival God, and killed his faith in doing so. He made that monster, and it killed his soul.'

'But you are not Gervaise. You are God's loyal servant.'

'He tempted me! He tempted me! The Devil saw the weakness in me, and now he has me in thrall, and God has gone!' His voice rises to a scream, just as the wind crashes and screams down the chimney, blowing soot and ashes into the room.

'What you are saying makes no sense. You are allowing your bodily exhaustion to affect your spirit. Even if you won't eat, you must take some rest. Sleep is the remedy for such moods, and you are in no state to discriminate between what is real and what is madness. God loves you, He made you, He is with you eternally, and forgives all sin.'

Kenneth presses his face into his hands and begins to sob.

Rowan feels pity for him, and a sense of his own powerlessness. For what man does not know despair? 'Stay with me here, if this place is so disturbing to you. You might lie down on the table here, out of the wet, and try to sleep. We can keep each other company: you have been too long alone.'

Kenneth wipes tears from his eyes. 'The loch will burst its banks if it keeps on raining like this. Then we shall be trapped with the evil spirits that walked here before we came.'

Looking out of the window, Rowan sees that the sky is lowering black, and the rain is still coming down in torrents, swelling the dark waters of the loch. It is true that they must leave as soon as possible, but he has no choice — he must complete his task.

'Look — Kenneth, I understand very well how much ...'

But when he turns, Rowan sees that he is standing in an empty room.

XX

The witches soon make good their promise. A visit from King Duncan: an unlooked-for honour. And an opportunity that must be taken. Among his tall men he is a frail and slender figure, commanding attention with his quiet voice. His bodyguards are seven feet tall, and do not speak. Prisoners, she learns, from some exotic victory. He speaks with the retainers, even the pot boy and porter, listening carefully. When they have eaten, he sends away the minstrels and storytellers, and instead he tells old tales himself: some of heroism and great battles, of Fionnghall, and the Clann Morna, and Goll mac Morna, but also of the winter goddess Beira, who raises storms and blizzards, conceding power to Brighid at Beltane in the spring. These stories make the hair prickle on Wulva's arms; she knows them in her bone and marrow.

At last, the King calls for lights to show him to his chamber. The room comes alive again, and Macbeth is smiling, bowing, showing his royal guest the way, along bright passages, sconces ablaze with new-lit candles. Duncan's room is adorned with silks and velvets, hangings from China and Damascus, lately purloined from Elgin castle.

They lie together. She whispers in his ear, not her words, but those of Cailleach. Goaded by her own horror of what he is and what he craves, by visions of blood and death and war, she makes him prey. A plan. A goal. A murder. How to fell the bodyguards and blame them. Giants slumber as peacefully as dwarves if they are drugged. And their wine has been attended to; she has seen to that already. When she pauses, she can still hear Cailleach, spooling promises. He shrinks from her, and turns his face away. She wraps herself around him, loads him with her great-belly, gently strokes his flaccid cock. What a man you are, my lord! The skin between them melts and merges — they are one creature, which must have what it most craves. His strength restored, he'll do it.

The room is black and silent. Time looms; she marks each step that he must take, the route from this place to the royal chamber. She sees Duncan as clearly as if she were standing in the room. He has no time to scream; his neck is severed, and blood pumps on the silken cover. She sees the kick and quiver of his veined legs, feels the jolt of his soul's passing, shocked and reeling, freed to go. She lies quite still, like a corpse herself. Her deed is done. The mormaer comes again, all ripe and bloody. She greets him as the King.

It's real, it's done, and Macbeth will rule. She can scarcely believe her bargain with the witches was accomplished with such ease. Great turmoil when they arrive at Scone, a melee of strangers, calls, instructions. Wulva is shown to a solar that seems to her as big as a church, hung with bright embroidered tapestries, and scented with lavender and hyssop. Ladies come and bathe her with rosewater. They are quiet, and keep their eyes downcast, as if she is not only too important to converse with, but even to look upon, as one must not look upon the face of Almighty God. There are sweetmeats and almonds, coloured jellies and spiced wine. And she eats *figs* from *Granada*. Neither of these words is known to her, the fig a soft fruit with seeds that crunch between her teeth, Granada, she supposes, a far-off place, imagining gold sun and roaring lions. Such ease and luxury is now her due, but it makes her uneasy: she can hear the clamour and activity of the men from where she reclines, and Macbeth with them, doing what must be done in preparation for the crowning. Meanwhile, her sole preoccupation is the hour at which she'll have her hair washed and braided. She wonders if it is always thus with queens, or whether her lord and master has decreed that she must be lulled with treats, kept busy in pursuit of the exquisite. He knows, as she does, that she has smoothed his path and stiffened his resolve. She sips the wine, and eats the almonds, and tells the ladies they can wash and dress her hair that afternoon.

Wulva considers the person in the mirror. The hard look in the eyes, the sharp bones, the firm-set lips. She had thought herself a gentler creature, once, when she lived with Aefric and little Cormac. But those days are long gone. She holds her own dark gaze. The mirror is meant to serve her, but she fears it is the other way about. Then gowns and lengths of stuff appear, borne by her ladies; fittings commence for coronation robes; she's a doll, decked out in stiffened, scented finery.

Macbeth is crowned. The people are crowded into the abbey like red hens in a winter coop. If anyone has doubts about the way this coronation came about, no one is saying so. Fear is her husband's greatest ally: his men are lined up at the front, their swords left at the church door, but not far away, propped against the wall. As for what thoughts are in his mind, he is giving nothing away. His face is a white mask; his eyes are fixed on some distant point, a future, perhaps, when he will be certain that what he has now can be secured for good. At the end of the ceremony, he takes her hand. His flesh is colder than a sepulchre.

After they are established at the royal seat of Dunsinane, Macbeth seems further from her still. Chill winds blow through the castle, and terror stalks its halls and chambers. There are newcomers who keep their faces covered, lurk in the shadows, eat at the far end of the table. Unsettled, the ladies whisper tremulously when they think she cannot hear, but her ears are sharper than they realise. These strangers are recruits to the King's expanding army, and more men come each day. Hardened from campaigns no one has heard of, bearing scars and mutilations and faces burned by distant sun. Few are admitted to his presence, just a small cadre of his trusted men. The light in his chamber burns till dawn.

His food is tested by his body-servant, and three men guard him, keeping their weapons with them at all times. Macbeth himself carries his broadsword with him, as though even his trusted servants might betray him. Sometimes he strides along the battlements, as if on the lookout for attackers. Not satisfied with what he sees, he commissions his workmen to build a new curtain wall, constructed from the strongest oaks in Birnam Wood. Only the tallest and most magnificent trees are fit for this construction. Hundreds of ancient trees are felled, and pale clearings appear in the woodlands like patches on a balding head. When the work is done, the wall is surmounted by great wooden spikes, so the castle looks like the spoked crown of an elvish king.

Next, with the agitation of a madman, the King decides

he must have a moat, as if the hilltop situation of the castle and its new wall are not sufficient to defend it. Five hundred workmen are commissioned, who camp outside the walls. They dig a deep trench round the castle, and a canal to connect the new moat to the nearest river. The moat fills up with brackish, discoloured water. This great workforce must be provided for, so the cellars are stacked with barrels of beer and salted eel, and dried carcases and cheeses are hooked up in the kitchens. Macbeth decrees that battle-ready men must have copious fresh meat, so sheep and cattle are herded into the outer court, ready for slaughter. So many are killed that the castle reeks like a tannery. Still restless, the King mobilises his waiting troops as huntsmen. They ride into the forest with whoops and war cries, armed with bows and arrows, knives and broadswords, laying waste to all the animals they find, returning with carcases by the dozen: foxes, deer, beavers, poll cats, badgers, wild boar, and wolves. Fresh hides for everyone, cloaks and tunics, coats and leggings; every bed in the castle now has an extra coverlet, and the floor of the solar is covered with the skin of the greatest kill of all, a black wolf of such monstrous size that it was thought he might be a creature out of fable. No one but Wulva seems to see that the castle is now filled with death. When she goes into the forest with her ladies — sedate, astride a palfrey, weighted down by her fine dress — she finds the woodland scorched and ravaged, with burned tracts where the hunters lit their fires. Lying among the dead trees and trampled bracken are the rotting corpses of the creatures they left behind: so many were killed that they could not bring all the trophies home.

Wulva has never felt as alone as she does now. The witch's pictures of the future may come to be, but she lives in the present moment, with her conscience. With guilt comes fear: the tale that Duncan was murdered by his body-servants is never openly questioned, but she wonders how many people truly believe it. At night she's watchful, sleepless, listening as Macbeth paces to and fro. She feigns sleep, not wanting to share this with him, this watching of the still black hour. One night, she's so disturbed she wanders onto the battlements, sucking the cold air into her lungs. When the servants come to find her, she pretends that she was walking in her sleep, that madness beckons. Yet her mind was never clearer. To avoid evil she has made a pact with evil, and her hands cannot be clean.

The new King sits with his advisors, some new, some from the old administration: he needs their knowledge, and they prefer to keep their heads. Macbeth is restless, sleepless, snaps at all who speak to him. But there is one man he does listen to, and whose counsel he respects: Griogal, a man whose lineage is unknown. Troll-like in appearance, he hogs the fireside, heavy-wrapped, and wears a hood pulled low over his face. The warriors and scar-cheeked hard-men pay attention to him, for Griogal has great schemes for winning battles, having studied the art of combat and consulted many martial tomes. Does he suspect Macbeth of seizing power? He gives nothing away, but he has an air of sinister omniscience.

There are long meetings around a carved table. These last for hours, sometimes going on deep into the night. Plans and schemes are mooted, men and horses are sent on missions. A new armoury is built. Yet still Macbeth is not satisfied. Still he cannot rest. One night, a stormy, wild night, he leaves their bed and disappears. She hears a horse clatter out of the courtyard far below, and wonders where he's gone and who he's seeking at this hour.

He returns at dawn, bringing in the cold of wind and heath.

'Out at this hour?' she asks.

'There is business to attend to.'

'You are King now; surely there are men who can assist you.'

'The only true man I have is Griogal. The others are all schemers.'

Why he places his trust in Griogal, she cannot say. He seems to her the least trustworthy of them all. 'Where did you go?' she asks.

He shakes his head. 'Once on the throne, there is nowhere to go but down. Death or deposition — that's my future. Or so I feared. But now, I find that I am safe from all who seek to harm me. I can't die from the cut of a man from woman born.'

She knows then what he seeks — this has the mark of Cailleach on it. Dissembling, she says: 'Then rest easy, sire. Lie down with me awhile.'

'Perhaps I should.' But he makes no move to join her.

'If you cannot die by a man's hand, then surely you will die an old man in your bed?' She thinks of Duncan, and wishes she had chosen her words differently.

He gazes at her, his eyes blank. 'There are vipers lurking round every corner, after my throne, hungry for blood. I must keep ahead of them.'

'God save us, sir. This is a fearful way to live.'

'No one asked for your opinion on this matter. Bring a healthy son to birth, and your work's done.'

She dozes, then wakes with a start. She dreamed that she was running with her jaws wide apart, roaring. She caught something, tore it open, sinew, gristle slipping from her claws. So clear is the memory that she looks at her fingernails, expecting them to be stained scarlet. They're white and clean. She sniffs her hands; no scent of blood.

But when she gets out of bed, she is wracked by pain, a cold, searing ache that bends her double. She screams, her women come to help her, and it begins — the black madness, wave upon wave, invades and weakens her. When it abates she can think and speak quite clearly, though there is nothing in her mind but dread. A midwife comes and tells her this is normal, the pain will worsen, but in the end all will be well. Wulva knows her certain tone is meant to soothe her, not to reveal an actual truth. The midwife does not speak of the times when such pain is the last thing a woman knows, she does not acknowledge that humans do not give birth as horses do in the field: easily, quickly, producing young that stand and walk just moments later. No, the bairn's head is always too big to come without great risk, and a woman must split in two to let it free. Then the child, a fat white tadpole, lies helpless in the crib thereafter, bleating for its mother's milk.

Wulva thinks of God the Father, who put Jesus into the body of Mary by means 'immaculate'. Nothing was written about how he came into that manger, what the travail was like for his mother, how long it lasted, how Joseph fared as her sole midwife. Did God send an angel to ease His Son's way? The Bible writers did not think such details were important, whoever they were. Men, of course; that much is certain.

The black fog of pain comes down and obscures the vision she has of a scholar with a white beard, writing with a quill. In its place, she sees the vastness of the forest, sweeping this way and that way around her, as if she is being dragged along among the trees. There is a singing and howling all about her, unlike anything that she has heard; she thinks that the souls in Hell might sound something like this, and tries to fathom where she might be. The blackness becomes a great tunnel ahead of her; she hurtles towards it, and the sound of screaming grows louder still. She's sucked into a void that spins and writhes, twisting like spilled guts.

She tries to cry out to the midwife, asking her to help, to draw her back, but what comes out of her body is a guttural roar, not a human voice at all. She tries again, putting all her might into pushing and calling, and sees that there is an opening up ahead, a small point of light. It gets bigger, and she sees the midwife and the solar, light angling through the windows. She is in the room again, and the scream is human, it's hers. But someone else is screaming too, and a voice is crying, 'Who will tell the master?'

There is a bundle with a bairn in it. The bairn is crying. Lusty, hearty, what a sound! The babe is healthy. The dread she felt subsides.

'Give him to me!' she cries, because she knows it is a boy, as Macbeth demanded. But the midwife turns away, clutching the crying babe.

'Give me my son!' screams Wulva.

She struggles to her feet and grabs the swaddled baby, holding him to her breast. She looks down at his face, and gasps with joy. The love is instant. He is a beautiful cub, with round yellow eyes and soft down on his snout. This, this is what they made, in that wild night! How could it have been anything else? A miracle, perfection. God has smiled on her, and Scotland will be ruled by wolflings. It takes a moment for her mind to note this: a hirsute, long-jawed prince was not expected.

The door slams open, a gusty roar, Macbeth fills the room. His shadow falls across her, the babe's unwrapped. Revealed, she sees her infant's beauty still, but the dread returns. His skin is covered with soft black hair; his pointed ears are flat against his head. The baleful wonder of him strikes her dumb.

Macbeth cries out: 'What in God's name have you done?'

Lifting the wolfling by its hind legs, he swings it hard, smashing its head against a wall post. Wulva screams and tries to wrench it from him, but he knocks her to the floor. Again he swings the bloodied, wailing form, beating its skull to pulp.

'You witch,' he screams. 'You cursed hag, what foulness have you birthed me? How dare you bring such evil to the Crown?'

There's blackness, a void, and when she comes to, the wolfling's meat, his corpse twitching. Macbeth whirls the dead thing round and throws it on the fire.

XXI

Putting thoughts of Kenneth aside, Rowan works in the scriptorium till evening. The work is absorbing, and for a while he is immersed in a scholar's trance, a rhythm of reading and thinking, stopping only to light his beeswax candle and be momentarily startled by the brightness of its light. He is not concerned now with its purpose, or with Father Andrew and his ambitions: the work is enough unto itself. At the end of the day, he stops, stretches his aching back, and returns to the present moment. He walks solemnly back to the chapel, thinking that he can, at least, promise Kenneth that he is reaching the end of his labours.

But the chapel is empty. He stares down the long nave at the two images of Christ, crucified and risen, and the wind shrieks though the broken windows. He shields his candle from the draught, wrong-footed for a moment, as he had been so certain he would see Kenneth's kneeling figure there. He returns to the solar, where he is relieved to see that Kenneth's pack and clothes remain: at least he hasn't left without him. Anxiety mounting, he makes another search of the abbey. Kenneth seems close by; he feels his presence. Sometimes he thinks that he hears running footsteps, a scuttering, like someone rushing up a flight of stairs. Sometimes he thinks he hears Kenneth singing, but when he stops to listen, it is only the sound of the incessant rain. His flickering candle shows up vistas of wet stone, looming fresco-faces, deserted rooms. He calls and calls until his throat is hoarse. But there is no reply.

He goes to the great door and looks out at the descending rain. The mountainside is all but obscured, its peaks rising coldly from the mist. He feels utterly alone. With a heavy heart, he returns to the solar and eats the last small piece of bread, hungry but swallowing with difficulty. What can be done? His friend's mind is disturbed; it's possible that he has concealed himself somewhere. And he is exhausted; perhaps he's fallen asleep in some sheltered corner? But Rowan has a growing sense of dread.

When he wakes in the morning, Rowan sees with a pang that he is still alone. Recalling Kenneth's distress, he wonders if he should have done more to help him. But it is his Christian duty to continue with his labour. He tramps around the abbey once again, hoping that the daylight might assist him. Again he calls for Kenneth, but the only sound is the returning echo.

In the scriptorium, there is water trickling down the walls. Would that he had built an Ark, like Noah, and could load the remaining documents aboard. Barrels of parchment instead of beasts. He takes out the documents and restarts his work. But he realises, as he begins again, that the words on these documents are more difficult to read. It seems that, even in one night, the pages have become more blurred and indecipherable. Where he left off yesterday, there are no legible words at all, just a foul-looking carbuncle, stained dark with oak-gall. He stares, frowning, then looks up at the roof over his head. There is no sign that water is coming from above. So how has this happened so quickly? That sense of evil and threat that Kenneth has spoken of — is it possible that there is something present here, something that haunts the empty chambers and passageways? He puts the thought aside. What absorbs him, more than the present condition of the abbey, is what is lost already, all those volumes and sources ruined beyond redemption. His work is like that of a surgeon on the battlefield: repairing what remains, making what he can of the shattered and broken. He frowns at the wording on the document he has found — more kings, more begat, begat, begat. *Is this history*, he wonders, *or a breeding catalogue? Are we men or prize cows?* All men know, even unworldly monks, that a man takes his own fathership on trust; it is only the woman who can lay claim to her children without a doubt in her mind. Great kings pass through the body of the dam, even though she may be nameless in the record.

His careful notes now start with Alpín mac Echdach, but he has only just got to the house of Dunkeld and its first ruler, Donnchadh mac Crionain. The section on the next ruler, Mac Bethad mac Findlaích, is particularly badly damaged, the surface of the parchment swollen like a tumour, so the writing is stretched and distorted. Indeed, the damp seems to have returned to the parchment something of its previous animal life, so that he feels as if these precious records are written on an exhumed corpse, rotting even as he writes. He stares, bemused, at the words. Mac Bethad, is that the spelling? Somewhere else in the document he saw this shortened to 'Macbeth'. There is a wife — the name beginning with 'Gru' — and then another under, but he can't make that out at all. Mac Bethad's dates are illegible. The sound of dripping is relentless, and his ink is slower than a creeping slug. He writes on, compelled, until he gets to the end of the Dunkelds — Alasdair mac Alasdair — and gives up when he gets to the next section, which appears to concern a woman named Maigread from Norway, but which makes no sense at all. He lifts up the document to look closer, and it falls apart in his hands, the lost names collapsing into pulp. He sighs: there is no alternative but to make the best of it he can. Touching the rest of the documents as little as possible, he arranges them in logical order and makes a new copy, creating sense and pattern out of confusion.

He writes and writes, copying the words in his elegant hand, the knowledge written by the dead, long-forgotten brother coming through his pen as juniper liquor drips through a still. The rhythm of his work becomes instinctive, and he feels as if the sound of the rain is connected to the moving quill. As he works, he wonders how people shall ever recover what's missing. So much of his own life has vanished, even from recollection. His childhood is a chain of vibrant images, like abbey windows. Was he really once a snotty boy, running and scavenging, making fools of other children, falling in the mud? It's not possible to know this boy; he can't get back to him. And these kings — finding new life now in the black ink — even their records are chaotic, drowned, besmirched. But out of this he must appease the longing for true facts, pure clarity, the truth. He works on, the lines slowly growing in number.

He comes to the end, having completed this work to the best of his ability. He stops, lays down his pen, feeling as if he has woken from a long sleep, dreaming of the great Saints and the green hills of his homeland. The scriptorium is in shadow. Looking out of the window, he sees that it's almost evening. The sky is lowering, dark clouds press down on the mountaintops, and the loch is shimmering black. The waters have reached the level of the window, and a slow trickle is rolling over the stone sill. Gathering up his parchments and his writing pouch, he hurries out. Kenneth must be somewhere; he can't have vanished into thin air. Rowan scours the halls and corridors, mounting staircases, opening door after door, reasoning that searching the same places makes sense, if his troubled friend is wandering witless around the monastery. 'Kenneth!' he calls. 'Where are you? I have finished, we can leave now! We can go!'

Here is the secret garden, a garden without entry or cloister. He looks down at the three yew trees, and the flourishing plants and flowers, the climbing vines, the lush entanglement. He leans out of the window, trying to see a way in, but fails. If Kenneth is unhappy, then this place might soothe him. He calls again; the yews sway in the wind, the flowers are folded in on themselves, their colours muted. The only way he can enter is to leap from the window, and then he will have no way to leave. He sees its beauty, but this time he feels its wrongness more strongly, and closes the window.

He is confused. He sits down, composes himself, and starts again, this time consulting the list he made when he first came to the monastery. He must follow a system; he must be thorough. He starts again, marking each one off, empty and checked: chapel, chapter house, warming room, dormitory, cloisters.

After searching the sacristy, he turns a corner and finds a door he had not noticed previously. It is odd that he hasn't seen it. When it creaks open, he sees a long flight of stone steps leading down into a void — the cellars. He does not wish to go down there. 'Kenneth?' he calls. 'It's Rowan. I've finished my work! We can leave tomorrow, at first light.' Then, thinking how ritual reassures his friend, he adds: 'After Lauds!' But there is only silence: yawning, empty silence.

He does not wish to go down there, yet he must. If he does not, his search is incomplete. Who knows what state Kenneth has got himself into. He may be lying injured. The thought of him dying in the cellar, incarcerated, is too horrible to contemplate. Rowan says a short prayer to God — another of his unofficial, selfish ones — and descends the staircase. When he gets to the bottom, blackness looms, and when he moves the candle around, he can see that the floor is flooded. 'Kenneth?' he calls again. He steels himself and wades into the freezing water. Instead of calling out for Kenneth, he now finds that all he can say is the Lord's prayer, in the Latin: *Pater noster, qui es in caelis, sanctificetur nomen tuum* ... The words recede and echo in the vast chamber. He wades forward, trembling. The cold is bitter, eerie, and chills him to the bone. In the candlelight, he sees anterooms, curved ceilings, long passageways like underground rivers. His prayers are trapped beneath the earth, as he is. He wonders if the dark passages might lead to the dead monks' crypt. Then he hears another sound — is it someone crying? He tries to place it, and knows that he is listening to the last screams of the pig-man.

XXII

There is only darkness after this. Her power has gone, his lust is spent, the wolfling's burned upon the fire. No burial, no last rites, no place in Heaven or Hell for such a monster. Yet was he so unnatural, after all? He came from her, fed from her body, his limbs folded inside her. In the fog that fills her mind, she is not sure if this is how it was, or there is some other story of how it came out. She cannot think, she cannot even dream. Food sticks in her throat, and her face in the obsidian mirror is a skull. She hardly dares to speak, lest she let out a howl.

Somehow, she keeps up a pretence of being as she once was. A stillbirth is a common mishap, as is the death of a newborn, and the mother will keep to her room as she would do after any ordinary birth. Therefore, Wulva must conduct herself as if this is one of those small tragedies that every mother knows. Luck is on your side if you survive childbed, and a healthy child to suckle is a bonus. Only Macbeth, she herself, and the midwife know of the mis-birth. And the midwife, perhaps in fear of her life, disappeared that night. Macbeth has put out word that she is possessed by Lucifer, and her word cannot be trusted.

Wulva attempts daily life, ties her wimple tightly round her head, attaches the heavy bunch of household keys to her belt, goes from room to room, with orders, requirements, tasks to accomplish. Stillness and silence are her enemies. Horror and terror stalk her only when the light has gone. Then nightmares come.

The wolfling's birth might be unmentionable, but the fact of it has changed Macbeth. He still wants to lie with her, but is savage, bestial, vicious. This blackness of deep night consumes them. She wishes she could cease to be. When they've finished, he doesn't sleep, but sits at the window, staring at the black. In the daytime, he keeps his distance, but she knows what he's about — scheming, plotting, sending hired killers out to do his will. Their best servants make their excuses and move on. The castle fills with scoundrels, chancers, mercenaries, men who sense the potential of advancement in the household of a warlord with night fears and a thirst for blood.

There is nowhere in the land that Macbeth does not fear. The more spies he has in his employment, the more rumours of insurrection come to his notice. Old friends are a menace to him, because they know too much. Strangers are a threat, because their minds are closed to him. Wulva fears that this bodes ill for Macduff and the family who loved her. And for her own part, she longs for what she once called home. She longs to see Aefric's face again, for the bustle and laughter of the

Macduffs' great hall, so different from the hushed and urgent muttering that fills Dunsinane. Perhaps she might share her fears with Aefric; perhaps her stepmother might advise her, as she did when she was young. Most of all, she wants to be sure that Aefric and the children do not come to harm.

'I wish to go to the Macduffs,' she says to Macbeth.

He nods, paying scarcely any attention. 'Of course, of course. Do as you will.'

'Did you hear me, sir? I want to go away, to stay with my family. And I must go soon, before the weather turns.'

His eyes harden. He has heard her properly now. 'You have no family but me,' he says.

'Please give me your permission, sir.'

He stares at her, mollified by this apparent timidity. 'It is a dangerous journey, and a long one. You need protection. Griogal will lead your party.'

Of all the henchmen at the court, it is Griogal she fears the most, with his air of infinite quietness and his narrow, calculating gaze. Even with this restriction, though, she is relieved that Macbeth has agreed to let her go. She wonders if, in his heart, he wishes to be free of her for a while. Perhaps her presence afflicts him just as his afflicts her.

Her spirits lift when they leave the confines of the castle, and she sees open country lying ahead. The journey is pleasant, and the only impediment to a passing happiness is the presence of Griogal, who does not join in the conversation, pays no attention to the stories the courtiers tell, and takes no part in the singing. She would think him snakelike if she did not have such a fondness for snakes. Long ago, in the great forest, she once made a study of the viper. The witches were partial to a snippet of its tongue for their concoctions, but she also learned to track it through the undergrowth, and wait for hours, so she could watch it kill its prey. Deadly as it is, the viper has an elegance and beauty that Griogal cannot lay claim to.

The castle of the Macduffs comes gradually into view, familiar and comforting. She rejoices to see the cluster of small barns and cottages that surrounds the castle, and the vegetable gardens and cow-pastures that hug its walls. Cottagers wave as they pass by. Smoke is rising from the chimney of the great hall, and when they ride into the courtyard, stable boys come grinning to meet them, and women call from the upper windows. Wulva looks up to see blossoms of white laundry drying in the sun. She remembers wash-days so well: the ordered chaos, the frenzy of fighting dirt with lye, and how she'd laughed when she discovered that it was itself a paste of ash and piss. Macbeth's castle is ordered by its men; Macduff's castle is ordered by its women. She did not understand its femaleness when she lived there, for she had nothing to compare it to. Now the contrast strikes her forcefully.

Aefric runs over and embraces her. 'My dear love,' she says. 'How I've missed you.' She stands back. 'You're thinner. Come inside and eat.'

They enter the fiery uproar of the kitchen. A loud argument is underway, which appears to be about the comparative merits of a route through the great forest. No one is convinced by any path other than the one they have always followed, yet all of them admit to having been lost many times. The cook remains aloof from the discussion, but after a while she says, with great authority, 'Let each man find his own way to Hell,' which seems impossible to answer.

Aefric fetches cakes and apples, ignoring the cries of the servants insisting that they could bring a platter to her, and they go up to the solar, where Cormac is playing. For a while they speak of familiar things. Then, hesitating, Wulva tells Aefric that she's lost a bairn.

'A stillbirth?' asks Aefric, gently.

She is on the brink of telling all, but fear defeats her. 'It lived for a little while.'

'God rest its little soul! I'll pray that it might find its way to Heaven. You will have others. Often, very often, the first one does not thrive.'

'Yes.'

Something in her face betrays her. Aefric puts her hand on her arm and says: 'I hope Macbeth — the King — I hope he's good to you. He was insistent, you see, even though I thought it strange, to summon you, having scarcely spoken ...'

Wulva chooses her words carefully, clouding the truth

with lies. 'It is all as it should be. I have no complaints at all.'

Aefric hugs her tightly. 'I know how much it hurts to lose a bairn. But see me now, my children all around me! There is no greater wealth. And as for husbands, well, many's the woman would have set her cap at Macbeth when his wife died. He is a proper sort of man, and has a way about him.'

'Yes, of course,' says Wulva. She smiles. But so much is left unsaid. The love she felt for her newborn was like nothing she's ever known. She felt no revulsion at the sight of it, and why should she? Her wolf cousins looked just the same. It grieves her that she can't confide in her stepmother as she used to. She can see that Aefric views Macbeth differently now that he's her monarch and linked in marriage. It is easier for Aefric, as for others, to think him worthy of the throne. Wulva wishes that she could live in that world of fairy tale, in which Macbeth was her true love, a wise King, and a new bairn would restore them.

'You must regain your strength now. You will only recover your spirits when you have a healthy new bairn,' says Aefric. 'Have one of these cakes. They're very good; Cormac helped make them.'

Wulva kisses Cormac, and he squirms away, laughing and wiping his cheek.

'Any new words for me, little one?' she asks, looking at his hornbook.

'Termnasc,' he says, fiddling with his chalk.

'I never heard it!'

'It's a bandage on the toes and thumbs of a dead body, to stop his ghost from hunting foes.'

'A worthy word, most useful.'

'And stravaig.'

'What's that?'

'Wandering about without knowing where to go.'

'That one I'll use, I'm sure.'

'And also some words for the Devil —'

'Really, Cormac!' says his mother. 'That is not fit work for a little boy.'

'But they are fine words,' he says. 'Auld Clootie, Auld Hornie, and Plotcock.'

'That is enough,' cries Aefric. 'Wulva, you see how they are running amok without —' She looks uneasy. 'Go and find your brothers, we've had enough of you in here.'

'Sweet boy!' says Wulva, watching him go.

'I know a mother shouldn't love one child more than another, but my heart goes out to that one. I don't know how he will fare in the great wide world; he's such a dreamer.'

'He will be a poet,' says Wulva, decisively.

Aefric shrugs and smiles, seeming close to tears.

'My lord perhaps keeps him in order. Is he out hunting?'

Now Aefric avoids her eye. 'Oh, he's not here today.'

'When will he return? I shall be glad to see him! With your leave, I hope we may stay for a few days.'

'He's away.' Aefric looks down, frowning.

'Oh! Where has he gone?'

'On pilgrimage.'

'Where to?'

'So many questions, Wulva!'

'But where? Which holy site? Has he gone far?'

'Oh, yes, of course. To Canterbury.'

'Canterbury — all the way to England? It's a strange time to leave you here alone.'

'Why strange?'

'There is much turmoil, since the late king —' She breaks off. 'I don't know exactly. It just seems a little neglectful, perhaps.'

'I'm hardly alone. I have a household of doughty servants! He's offering his prayers to God for our safekeeping.'

'Would he not serve you better here? In his own person?'

Neither woman says anything for a moment, and there is a new coolness between them. Then they talk of what has changed since Wulva left, and for a while it seems as if ordinary things can hold their place. But Wulva is distracted, and her sense of foreboding is growing as they speak. She can scarcely believe that her stepfather has left his family and gone away on pilgrimage. And if he is away on some other business, what business might that be? Her thoughts race. She wonders if Griogal is here not only to keep an eye on Macbeth's wife, but to spy on her hosts? Her blood chills when she thinks of that cunning, whispering lackey. The doubts and fears that she had not quite identified before now come to the surface. She sees, now she is not at Dunsinane, the threat that it represents to those whom Macbeth sees as rivals.

'I think that you should leave without delay,' she says, lowering her voice.

'What? Why do you say so?'

'Go and join my lord Macduff.'

'Leave? God's teeth! I live here, Wulva. This is my home!'

Wulva tries to organise her thoughts. How much can she say? Might Griogal be listening at the door? She knows that she must be careful, yet also that she must seize this chance, and warn Aefric if she can. 'I am not sure if the King's quite well.'

'What is wrong with him? No one has spoken of his being ill. Is he in danger? Are doctors bleeding him?'

'Shush! Keep your voice down. Nothing that requires the attendance of a doctor. It's more that ... he is troubled in his mind. The duties of the Crown sit heavily on his shoulders, he is subject to sleeplessness, he worries ...'

'Surely that is natural?'

There is nothing natural about this, thinks Wulva. 'He sees a threat in every shadow! He cannot rest, and he mistrusts even his own men. There is fear abroad at Dunsinane, and it can only spread.'

'But what fear? What are you speaking of?'

'Of treachery and ... vengeance.' She wonders if already she has said too much.

Aefric hesitates. Wulva sees that they are both playing the same game, of cloaking lies of omission in seeming candour. 'I must say, I feared this very thing,' Aefric says at last. 'My lord — he will be back soon, but I don't know exactly when. He has a great love for the King, of course! But ... what are we to anyone?' She shakes her head.

Wulva takes her hand. 'Listen ... These are dangerous times, and things will worsen, I am sure of it.'

'But *leave*, how shall I *leave*? The safest place for me is here, behind these battlements.'

'Whatever the difficulty, that is the wisest thing to do.'

Aefric gives her a shrewd look. 'You are frightened of the King.'

'I never said so.'

They stare at each other, caught between love and fear.

'If things are as you say, then could you not speak to him on our behalf?' asks Aefric. 'He and Macduff were like brothers in their youth. Though that is a long time ago now.'

'I have no power with Macbeth. I wish I had.'

'Has he spoken of Macduff?'

'Not in my hearing. But everything is secret, hidden. Dear Aefric, please listen to me. *Leave*. Gather the boys, tell them some explanatory tale, and head south, across the border. Please.'

'There are such perils in a journey. I will be going from the frying pan to the fire. If there is danger, then you must speak for me. I see no other way!'

Wulva leans forward. 'I tell you, Dunsinane reeks of blood. And fear. Lucifer stalks us, his agents sit with us at table. The King is looking for culprits, traitors, the weakest link in his domain. He suspects — I don't know what. Now my lord has gone, the King will think the worst, and that places you in mortal danger.'

'Surely you don't mean he would harm me or my children?'

'No one is safe from him, no matter what their age or station. Go where he can't find you. Leave at night if need be. Tell only those retainers whom you trust. I will make some excuse to my servants, return at first light, and do my utmost to assure the King that he has nothing to fear from you.'

Wulva knows that not a moment must be wasted. She leaves with her men at dawn, and they reach Dunsinane at nightfall the following day. As soon as they enter the courtyard, she sees that things have changed in the short time since their departure. The lights in the castle are blazing, and the courtyard is crowded with men-at-arms. She dismounts, descending into the fray.

'What's happening? What's going on?' But no one answers.

From the great hall, she hears the sound of shouting and breaking glass. Griogal rushes towards the stairway to the hall, and she follows. Macbeth is standing behind the high table, with his henchmen around him. The debris of a meal lies before them. Macbeth is on his feet, berating one of his officers, yelling and pointing, spittle flying from his lips.

'You fool, you fly-brained knave! Is there not a man here can be trusted? How am I so ill-served? Why is this castle filled with vipers, back-stabbers, traitors?'

'Sire, we have been vigilant, I swear,' cries the man.

'What is the matter, my lord?' asks Wulva. Again, no one answers. She hurries nearer, climbs onto the dais, and approaches the table.

Macbeth ignores her. But she perceives, with that intuition that serves her well, that the fear which has stalked her husband now has him in thrall, that he is mad with it. His face is white; his black eyes glitter with wild terror. 'Now you are here, Griogal, let's hear the news from Fife. I want to know who has betrayed me.'

Griogal bows obsequiously. 'Your Majesty, long may God protect you. Lord Macduff has fled to England to raise an army, as you rightly suspected. And following your further estimable instructions, once I discovered this, I was able to discreetly commission certain local assassins who proved amenable to payment for services to be rendered statim.'

'What do you mean?' cries Wulva. 'What services?'

'Did I give you permission to speak, you two-faced whore?' shouts Macbeth. 'Why do you think I gave you leave to visit that tribe in the first place? I knew Macduff could not be trusted. Be silent until I give you leave to address your monarch. Griogal, continue.'

'We agreed that they would enter the castle after our departure, to, ah, complete this transaction. We will soon have news of how it went, and proof of their dispatch. I see no impediment to its full success, given that my lord took off with most of his fighting men, leaving his coop and chickens unprotected. Exemplary assassins in that location, and most affordable. You can buy a murderer for half a pig.'

XXIII

Rowan is in the solar, folding up his pack. The sun is shining through the window; a mouse is sitting in the warm light. There is no pig-man, no screaming cellars; he is not lost, knee-deep in water. There is nothing to fear; the night is merely lightless, there is no evil in it. Man has perfect understanding of what must be understood, and God attends to those matters which are beyond the reach of mortal minds. What happened last night is explicable. Because these are trying circumstances. There is a great deal on his mind. Kenneth, allegedly his protector, has departed. But this need not concern him. He has no need of protection; he will pack his bag and go. All is well. All will be well. Parchment rolled at its centre — he knows this is important, like the kernel of a nut.

Try as he might, though, he can't sustain this clarity. He must put the parchment in his bag, then he must leave, but he is not sure of his purpose. He should be praying, but he is not sure of the hour. He is at the doorway, looking out. Mountains, sky, cloud. A clean wind. He grins into it, baring his teeth. *Away from this charnel-house*, he thinks.

Out of the Flood. No rain now, he sees, just clear wiped blue. When he was a boy, how he would have loved this day. Would have known how to use it, then. A child does not *use*, it *is*. When you are young, left to your own devices, a day is not a sequence, it is a space. That is the secret that one loses.

He sees now that the causeway is flooded. The waters of the loch have reached the abbey steps. God will save him, angels will bear him up. He wades in, sandals around his neck, balancing his pack upon his head, and cries out in pain at the coldness of it. Yet it does not restore his mind to order. But the angels, in their mercy, do save him from drowning; his feet remain on stony ground. Only Christ can walk on water. Mortal Rowan trips and staggers; the water ebbs around his legs. There was that other freezing water in the dark. Satan was there! He will not think of it. He will not run mad. Brother Rowan, in full possession of his wits. On ecclesiastic business. Practical reminder of his situation: sandals worn like a surplice, pack carried on the head. He thinks: *I am not Christ, I am a laundry woman!* And this strikes him as great wisdom — his pilgrimage has been worthwhile. He would rather carry laundry than kill the Infidel; he would rather write a monarch's name than meet one. On the other side, he weeps, for joy, for loss. He knows that he will not see Kenneth again.

When he reaches the lip of the high ground, the journey home seems to stretch ahead of him: he *perceives* the route he has to take, right up to the oak door of the priory. The way is brightly lit, Christ showing it to him with His lantern. The Christ has beeswax candles, the product of celestial hives. Only the brightest light for Christ the Lord! But he realises that this vision cannot be, and shakes his head. He must keep hold of his wits; he must not let his mind decay, like ruined parchments. That bubble and tear and crumble. That stink of mould and meat fat. He must hold fast. Not quite as he was, though. Not that little boy. The world now tipping, voiding, blurring. Kenneth, the king-line, the pig-man, and the dark. All in ceaseless ferment. So be it, he must still keep on. He proceeds, slithering, unsteady, across the rock.

There is a horse grazing on rough grass, and he sees that it is Hestia. She comes over and greets him, and they walk together, over the stones and heather, to the drove-way. The air is cold, and he tries to recall the season. As he walks, he scans the surrounding landscape. Nothing seems familiar but his mare, and he is grateful for her company. He makes no attempt to ride her, as she has neither reins nor saddle, and he is happier at her side. He walked beside her once before, a thousand years ago, and wondered what she thought of. Now his thoughts are full of horse, and hardly any man. He sees and feels the land, rising and offering, grass tussocks, pleasant thistles. He sees and feels the gushing stream, where one might drink, soft lips in cool mud. What a man might think of, he can't say. He is high up, far off, communing with a horse, the world all turf and sky and wind. Three crows circle far above him, and he squints up at them, trying to remember why they seem familiar. At nightfall, he sleeps in a coppice. It is freezing, but he sleeps soundly enough, waking with a shock to see his frosted breath. His limbs are stiff; his hands are blue. Hestia comes and blows on them, and he leans against her warm body to thaw his own.

There are mountains stretching into the distance. He has the sense that he is travelling at great height. Each mountain has a white mantle, and now the snow falls gently, softly, seeming kinder than the rain. He trudges on, each step taking him away from the library, and from Kenneth. Is it still raining there? Or is the loch now freezing over? In still, clear moonlight, wolves are watching him. Their howls rise in the stark night, ravenous and yearning; their eyes flash green and yellow.

At night, he fears the bodach. Out of the cracks in the rocks, he feels them returning, all those weird creatures from his childhood, the haunters and harriers, the bearers of ill will. God made all the world, but what was there before? There are creatures with no fear of the Bible, they've lived so long. In the Beginning was the Word ... and the Word was God, but Beginning is a word. Is Beginning God? And God Beginning? What went Before? The yellow eyes might know. Cold prevents his thinking; it is snowing into his mind, his skull an empty bowl, filling with falling whiteness.

A long, grey loch; thin cloud in a pale sky. If he reaches the mountain's end, then he can ask the way. He has conversations with the horse of which he has no understanding. There were people here long ago, who had the skill of listening to horses and understanding them, but he only knows Latin, and English, and certain sorts of Gaelic. He knows about the Ancients, wise men in southern lands; he has philosophy and information. He thinks of Socrates, but all he can recall of his great teaching is: 'Wisdom begins in wonder', which he learned as 'Sapientia incipit in admiratione'. For some time he puzzles over this, until after a while he sees footprints in the snow, and thinks they may be Kenneth's, but then he sees that Kenneth is accompanied by a hoofed creature, and for a moment he thinks this might be Satan, but then he notices the creature is four-legged, and he realises the footprints are his, and he and Hestia are together walking in a wide circle. They are not Kenneth's, because Kenneth is dead. He worries that he is going in the wrong direction; he must go back to the deserted monastery, and walk across the ice, and bury Kenneth in the garden. But he doesn't know the way backward or forward. He is merely walking.

Gawaine knew the way, and Beowulf. Galahad too; they all followed the direction of their quarry, be it Green Knight, Grendel, or Holy Grail. For him, no such clarity exists. He is more confused now than when he started, and he had no great clarity then. Kenneth, who seemed set on a right path of some kind, has wandered further from the Way than he has. He is mad, and dead — no need for both things, surely! Nothing makes any sense at all.

Ahead of him is a forest; his way is blocked by trees as far as he can see. Hestia advances, whiffling, curious. There will be more for her to eat in the deep woods than on the snowbound mountain. When they walk between the dark trees, he hears them whispering to each other, and feels the flinch of root-speak beneath his feet, and the footfall of the running deer, and hears an owl hoot, far off, in the cold.

'Kenneth?' he calls out. 'Kenneth, are you there?'

Although Kenneth is dead, that is quite certain, dead and unburied somewhere, Rowan prays he was not felled by his own hand, for that way there is no salvation. The Pope, who gave dispensation to the souls who died from plague unshriven, will make no such intervention for dead Kenneth. He will know neither purgatory nor Heaven; it would be better to have been born a worm, which truly moves from Earth to Earth, eating it, burrowing in its cool dark, dying to form its loamy perpetuity. So he prays that Kenneth has been killed: a slip, a drowning, a fall. Anything but self-destruction. He should go back. He is going the wrong way. He must bury Kenneth, give him a Christian burial, that at least. Then he remembers he is not going in any direction, he is merely walking. He pats the mare's neck; she is busy grazing.

He comes at length to a clearing in the trees. There is a queer smell, not unpleasant, and winter sun shines on the matted grass. Something rising, grey, transparent. There is a figure, sitting, turned away from him, tending a fire. The woodsmoke rising, slow, the far trees showing through it. The figure twists around, sees him. She beckons. It is the old crone from the mill.

XXIV

The sky is cracked with lightning, and a white spike rips the sky, showing the empty mountain, the sheep track, and the glittering sea beyond. She's riding hard, alone, through crashing rain. The destrier is Macbeth's, the fastest in the stable, but no beast can travel fast enough. The path is becoming a river; the horse slows down and sloshes through the mire. A herd of sheep appears, the frightened creatures bleating and running to and fro, crossing and recrossing the flooded track. Wulva's face is wet with rain, her mind filled with misery and self-blame. It is better, she knows, to think of nothing, to clear her mind of memory and fear. But it's impossible to do. She should have made Aefric prepare a carriage while she was there, should have stayed until she'd left the castle, should have travelled with her to the border. But who was to know there was so little time? She reaches the far side of the flooded path, and canters along the side of a tall black forest, which roars and cracks.

She rides through the night. Deepest black, a raging sky, the horse now slowed to a trot. From time to time it whinnies, protesting. The creature wants to know why they are not stopping to rest. No one drives a horse like this. She pats its neck. Rider and mount, they are soaked through, and the horse's hooves slip on the stony pathway. The black night holds her; she has no fear of it, only of what she might find when it is done. Busy, urgent thoughts go chasing on, even as the horse slows, as the journey seems to lengthen, and she fears she will never get there. A wolf running through the wood ahead of her, beating a path through briar and bracken. Aefric with a sheet in a high wind, laughing. The wind taking her veil, whipped right away, so her hair blows free, and she looks like a maiden. Cailleach, with her Bible, pointing out a useful psalm with one long yellowed finger. Wulva sleeps, still in the saddle. She wakes and does not know the hour.

By the time she reaches Fife, it's early morning, and the world's transformed. The storm has cleared, and the sky is banded pink and gold. Curlews are calling, the ground smells fresh, and the moor is bright with purple heather. Beyond this, rocks glow in the dawn sun, and the sea is calm. Cormorants loop and dive into the water. She closes her eyes in the warming sunlight, praying all will be well, that Griogal was bragging before his master, that the local men were merciful or tardy.

When she reaches the castle, there is utter stillness.

Her horse is walking slowly now, and she doesn't try to goad him on. They pass beneath the drawbridge — there is no gatekeeper, no one cries out to challenge her. She dismounts, enters the keep, and looks around, heart beating fast. Where once there was noise and bustle, there is empty silence. The silence beats in her ears. There is not a soul in sight. The only living thing is a young pig, snuffling in the mud. She dismounts and it scurries off, grunting shrilly. She thinks of Iochtar, all those years ago.

Wulva tries to call for Aefric, but her voice won't come. For a moment, she hesitates, listens once more, hoping that she might hear some human sound. But there is nothing, nothing. She goes into the kitchen. The long room smells of burned fat, and cinnamon. Bake-meats are scattered across the floor. Eddies of black smoke come from the oven. The fire is smouldering; a hare, half skinned, lies on the long table. A chase hound lies across the threshold of the great hall with its throat cut. There are upturned benches, broken windows, trenchers cast upon the rushes. When she mounts the stairway to the solar, she slips on what she thinks is rain-slime. Looking down, she realises that the steps are slicked with blood, dripping glutinously. Her body is so heavy she can scarcely move, but she mounts the last steps somehow, holding herself rigid. Through the open door, she sees them. The older brothers lie together, flung into a tangle, gored and mutilated. Gavin still has a dagger in his hand. Aefric is hanging, naked, from the rafters, grey tongue lolling from her mouth. Cormac is lying at her feet. His blue eyes are wide open, face contorted in his final scream. His hornbook, smashed to pieces, lies beside him.

XXV

The fire crackles; the crone is cooking something on a spit. A badger, it looks like, though he can't be sure. There is something in a pot as well; there's an aroma of onions and garlic. He realises after all this time that he is hungry.

'You took your time, Brother Rowan,' she says.

'Was I expected?' Confused, he thinks: *She has an excellent memory.* They never asked what she was called herself; it had not seemed necessary. Is it possible that he did tell her they would meet? He grasps and flounders, trying to recall.

'Expected, yes. That is one way of putting it. We are a long way from that roadside inn, I must say. And Brother Kenneth, of course, was never going to last the distance. You've done well. The mare's a far more amiable companion.'

'I'm sorry if I've kept you waiting. But if we did have an assignation, then it has slipped my mind.'

'It is good to see you, whatever the day and hour. And if you are confused, then that gives me satisfaction. I've been journeying for I don't know how many years now, sowing seeds of doubt. Far beyond my three-score years and ten. My mission is to spread uncertainty, you might say. Or, at least, to put a stop to *certainty*, which is the very Devil, the vice of closed and narrow minds. So I like to see a man befuddled.'

'Am I befuddled?'

'If you weren't, you wouldn't need to ask me. But your humility serves you well. You are a fine man, Brother Rowan, better than the common run of them.'

He sits beside the fire, and they eat. It is indeed roast badger — he had forgotten how good it tastes. Yet even his enjoyment of his meal can't fully restore him. His mood is trance-like. He tries to remember when he last ate, when it was he finished those final remnants in his pack. He turned down the food that Kenneth rejected, that he does know, yet he must have eaten something. But time has looped and twisted, and his thoughts and memories slip away from him. He eats too fast, so that the food sticks in his throat. Too much, too quickly. A bowl of porridge might have served him better. The crone eats heartily, spitting out gobbets of fat. When she is done, she wipes her face with her apron and drinks from a leather bottle.

'Care for a drop of ale?'

Rowan shakes his head.

'Go on, it will do you good. Don't be so squeamish.'

It seems churlish to refuse, so he swigs some down, and is surprised by the taste — something like meadowgrass and roses. He begins to take more notice of the old woman and the present circumstances. The snow has melted around the fire, and they are each sitting on a dry rock, while Hestia grazes at the clearing's edge. A nightingale is singing in the wood, and a fox comes sniffling by, seeming unafraid. There is a sense of peaceable companionship, and he has an odd feeling of affinity with her. Yet he is sure they met only once, travelling from the mill cottage to the inn. Didn't they? She rode with him, and Kenneth was impolite. Poor, dear Kenneth. He wishes he could think more clearly. Pictures emerge and fade away. He was on an errand, wasn't he? An errand for Father Andrew. The late sun and a flagon of red wine. It seems so long ago.

'Yet it is not so long, not by my reckoning,' says the woman. 'It feels as if it happened in the last half-hour.'

'I don't believe I spoke aloud.'

'You didn't need to. Your thoughts were written on your face,' she says.

'That is an extraordinary skill you have.'

'I've had some time to learn it, as I say. There are patterns in humans, which I've had the chance to study, seeing them come and go as I have done. We all pray for long life, but I can tell you, I have been cursed with mine. But I don't regret what I did. I don't care if I go to Hell.'

Rowan crosses himself. 'Do not say such things. God willing, you will have a place in Heaven once you have paid your dues in purgatory.'

'God willing, yes, thank you, Brother Rowan. You are a good Christian.'

'I hardly think so. I'm a sinner, and a coward, at the very least.'

She stretches her legs out, as she did at the fireside in that far-off inn. 'Now that Brother Kenneth is elsewhere, you might like to hear the tale that he denied you. This is my allotted task, you see. To tell this tale. To anyone who'll listen.'

'Kenneth meant no harm. He was afraid of his own nature, I believe, and we are wise to fear that. Temptation can take any form. However, I must admit, I'm curious. I'd like to hear it.'

'It is not for the faint-hearted. But as I said before, I can vouch for every word of this account, as there is not one jot of it that I did not see for myself. Some may gainsay it, and I can't force any man to believe what I am telling him, but if you doubt the tale, then you doubt my character. And I assure you, I'm an honest woman, no matter what my past sins have been.'

'Very well. I should like to hear it.'

She smiles and takes another swig.

XXVI

The world tilts and founders. She sees a pewter bangle, a tattered, blood-scotched dress. She retches, bending double. The silent room is filled with screaming; she sees the struggle, the knives, the rope around the neck. The flailing limbs, the pleading. But that is over. The deaths are done; it's finished. There is no help for them. Wulva slashes at the rope until Aefric's corpse drops clumsily to the floor. She arranges the body as best she may, combs the hair from Aefric's face, and lays her children around her before covering all of them with a bedsheet. Then she sets the room on fire, taking a torch from the wall. The straw on the floor takes flame quickly, licking higher and higher, leaping and scorching. She doesn't notice that her own hair is singeing until it hurts. She bats at her head and burns her hands. Looks at her blackened palms.

The pain awakens her. Something happens, something new.

There's an itching, starting with her thumbs. Her face, snorting out of itself, pulling her eyes outward, but she sees nothing, only blurred red shadows. Her fingers curl, sprout agonising claws. The itching spreads; her body's furred and long, her clothes are torn to shreds. A violent strength runs down her limbs, and she feels her heart expanding. Wulva sniffs the ground and smells his men. What name? Mormaer, Macbeth, King. Now she can speak; she lifts her muzzle, howls. The room reverberates, the windows shatter, the sky is black with birds.

Cailleach is there, barring the way.

'The battle's lost and won! Your task is finished. Who is this she-wolf? This is not our plan.'

'I am neither wolf nor woman, fish nor fowl. See how I can shape-shift.'

'In the Devil's name, what are you?'

'You told me once, none of their names fit you. Norn or Fury, Fate or Witch. Numerous and multiple, shifting and permeable. It seems that none of them fit me either.'

'Don't try to wrong-foot me with my own words.'

'I shall please myself. You don't own me. No one knows the rules or borders. All the rest is casting nets for clouds.'

Cailleach is spitting with rage. 'Shape-shifter you may be, but stay away from what we've wrought. Go into the forest, where there are others like you.'

'You sent me to that family, and you knew how it would end. You wanted me to love them, so I would learn their ways, and I did love them. I know there is such a thing as human kindness. Macbeth has set his face against it, but they aren't all like him.'

'We told you not to trust the kind ones. They just kill us slower.'

'Why should we be hell-bent on destruction? Why must we despair? There's magic in the mormaers, just as there is in you. Your way is not the only way, and humanity does not have to end.'

'Intemperate termagant! How dare you. We told you the plan, and you are our instrument. You would have died of cold and hunger in Birnam Wood if we had not taken you in.'

'Intemperate? No. But I shan't wait a thousand years. There is one score to settle now.'

She lopes away, down scarlet steps, out of the castle. The land roars open, heath and scrubland, mire and mountain. Here's a forest, wide and hungry, its green glades seething and whispering. Something is happening here: hers is not the only transformation. Unsure, she stops and cocks her head, trying to read the signs. But they're not known to her. There are sounds, at first so quiet and gentle that they might be prowling foxes or scuttling weasels. But this is different. Her great ears strain to listen as the noise grows louder, a hybrid murmuring, a thousand elf breaths on the wind. When she sees the first oak shake its branches, she begins to understand.

The branches move, a gradual untwining, the delicate

space between each tree changing shape. The moves are sluglike — she can barely see them — yet the tree is shifting inexorably. Leaves begin to fall as if children are scrumping apples, and Wulva looks up. As the leaves fall, the branches shift and rearrange themselves, finding a different shape. Birds rise up, furious, screeching, and flap away. The ground beneath her feet begins to undulate, and the mouldy earth is splintered by root-claws. She's so still, listens so hard, that she hears the forest thinking. Earth and air are charged with tingling messages.

A herd of deer runs headlong past her, crashing through the bracken, dark eyes glazed in panic. As they go by, she sees it clearly: the forest is uprooting itself. It has become a many-centred being, a moving force born of the bone-damp soil. She lopes among the trunks and saplings, dodging falling branches, leaping mud-choked streams, until she reaches the far side of the wood, and the path to Dunsinane. Here, she observes that the edge of the forest has inched forward, and is moving in the direction of the castle.

A dreamlike chaos follows. She runs towards the squat black castle, yet while she draws closer, she cannot leave the wood. It surges, wild and creaking, all around her. She is running fast, yet the forest is abreast of her. Time swerves and trembles, its patterns merge and blossom. Now they are awakened, the old trees can outpace a running wolf. There are oaks approaching the castle walls, beeches leering over the battlements, ash trees breaching the embankment. The battlement of new-felled trees that crowns the castle is changing too, remembering where it comes from. Dead trees begin to live again, to put on leaf and thorn. Stout trunks sprout branches whose infant twigs reach out to join hands with their invading kin. The forest swells, fattens, rises, the woken trees relentless in their quest. The screams of men are legion, but few remain to fight an enemy that kills with sap and root, that opens its grain to suck them into living tombs like immured heretics. They jump from the battlements and flee.

He's on his throne, gold circlet on his brow. That was his prize, that hollow trinket. The wildwood's curling up around him, blood and branches, screams of his dead men. She bounds towards him, slavering. He sees that she's both wolf and Wulva. His eyes are wide with fear.

'What kind of witchcraft is this?'

'The sort that they call nature, which lived before men came.'

'Vengeance, is it? That's what you're after?'

'Nature does not avenge. It eats. It lives. It dies. And yet survives. I'm hungry, and your flesh is smooth and white.'

He lifts his sword, but he's too slow. Her long jaws close on his soft throat; her teeth pierce bone and gristle. She feels the life spurt out of him, as once she felt his seed. While he is warm and twitching, she eats him, limb by limb, tears tender flesh from muscle. Then all that's left is pale bone and his screaming royal head.

XXVII

When Wulva has finished her tale, Rowan sits for a long time, watching the firewood crumple to ash. The forest is dark now, and a pale moon has risen. It's cold at his back, despite the warmth of the last embers.

'That is quite a story,' he says. He struggles for clarity, dazzled and sickened. 'But I must take issue with you, if you say it's true. The ending, for example, is symbolic. A metaphor, not factual.'

She nods. 'I would agree with you, except that I can still hear his screaming. Two hours it took to finish him.'

'Which sounds unpleasant, I grant you. Visceral it may be, but your account is quite implausible. Apart from all this ... *transformation* and so forth, there is the question of historical accuracy. I know from my late study that Mac Bethad mac Findlaích, abbreviated to "Macbeth", the king of whom you speak, died centuries ago. And furthermore, he died in battle, man to man, in the customary way.'

'Ah yes, that's right. So it is written.'

'And so, you cannot be that person, can you? Who ate Macbeth, while transformed into a wolf? Supposing *that* was possible! I can scarcely believe I am having this conversation. It's allegorical. None of it is *true*.'

'I told you I had travelled for a long time — did you not hear me? This is a story for the telling, not the writing. And I never told you what I was. I didn't say I was a person. My name is Wulva, and that is all you need to know.'

He dozes then, too flummoxed to argue further. When he comes to, an old she-wolf is stretched beside him, sound asleep.

Her story unsettles his mind further. All attempt at logical thinking founders. Next day, Hestia has vanished, and he leaves the forest, lonely and perplexed. He wanders for many weeks, living off the generosity of strangers. One day, to his confusion, he arrives at his destination. A grey monolith beside a churning river. Inside, there is the sound of plainsong, the odour of lavender and beeswax. Someone is baking bread. Here is a man called Father Andrew. Good day to you, Reverend Father, yes, I am rather weary. Although he knows this place, it is not familiar. He feels he is the wrong shape and size, too narrow, too wide, too small, too bulky. The inwardness makes him queasy, and he craves the open land. Horses think better. Old women may not be persons, they may be she-wolves. *Would you like to hear my story*? Yes, I would. The windows shimmer in the celestial colours of Our Lord, shining jewels upon the stone flags. A ruby slides across his foot. He gives someone the parchment with his notes.

A young novice has taken his place in the scriptorium: a raw-boned fellow, head full of snot, who makes what sense of these he can. Knowing what his masters want, he uses conjecture and supposition to make good the gaps and puzzles. It is fine work. The prior is satisfied. He displays the pristine document in the cloisters. When — at length — they show Rowan the completed work, he shakes his head, perplexed, and returns to his accustomed seat in the warming room.

'I can tell a tale,' he says, 'that will make you long for daybreak.' It is broad daylight when he says this.

He tells the same story over and over, and each time he tells it, he sees into the dark mist of his mind. Three spirits and a wolf-child, a crazed warlord and a walking forest. A king consumed, retaining just his head.

They turn away, sorry to see good Rowan, a gentle scholar, declined to a gibbering fool. The garden still comforts him; he sometimes takes a hoe and digs the ground, but often he is relieved of it, and they say, 'This is not where we put the cabbages, let this alone.' These words are murky; sometimes there is writing in the air, and voices come from ghost children.

It is not possible to say how often something happens

— forever, many times, long, long ago, or just the once, this moment, you are in the way.

One winter becomes another, the autumns merge and blur. In the here, it is another summer; there's bee-song, plangent and eternal buzzing, banks of strident flowers, the herb garden, sweetly aromatic, a cacophony of scents. He sits in the shade, watching others go about their busyness, and thinks about the past, and Kenneth, and that tiny room, with all that knowledge cased inside. What will survive of it? Painstaking marks on parchment, worlds and visions. Leaping creatures in the margins, twisted evocations of flower and forest, embroidering plain words. Latin, Greek, Aramaic. Then books are burned and shredded. He sees the years to come, the seeping damp, the bonfires, words consumed. The hag tale, where did that go? What was the story that she told him? He stares out at the dazzle, lost and wandering, a horse by his side, the mountains looming in the distance.

The seasons change. Leaves crimp and wither in the priory orchard. Three hooded crones walk slowly across a tundra of dead soil. The monks recede and sicken, the abbey tumbles into dust, there are new voices, chapters, kings. And then a silence. Ice melts, waters rise, the peoples move across the Earth like shadows. Clouds of insects rise from hell-pits. Oceans drown in poison. Deserts burst their banks and fill whole continents with burning sand. The sun shines down on barren fields, white and pitiless and blinding.

Acknowledgements

This book could not have been written without the help of the Society of Authors and the Authors' Foundation grant. Their generosity gave me the confidence to complete a novel which I knew would be strange and unusual, and which I had been mulling over for a decade. The work-in-progress grant allowed me to spend some time working on the draft at Moniack Mhor, near Loch Ness, the ideal setting for bringing the first draft of *Hagtale* into being. Many walks in the mist and encounters with medieval-looking sheep aided the process.

Writers who inspired me include Charles Foster (*Being a Beast*), Ronald Hutton (*The Triumph of the Moon*), Angela Carter (*The Bloody Chamber*), William Golding (*The Inheritors* and *The Spire*), Andrew Michael Hurley (*Starve Acre*), and James Meek (*To Calais, in Ordinary Time*). And of course, William Shakespeare, who transmuted dry historical records into the baleful Scottish play.

Thanks to my first readers, including Chetna Maroo, Fiona McWilliam, Hannah Vincent, and Georgia and

Declan O'Reilly, to Daisy Arendell and Jo Unwin for finding a home for this book, and to Joanna Swainson for her wise counsel. I'm also grateful to Molly Slight for her belief in this novel, and to the rest of the team at Scribe, especially Marika Webb-Pullman for her incisive editorial suggestions, and Jo Walker for the stunning cover design.

And finally, thank you, Noel, for putting up with my relentlessly high-maintenance approach to writing. You are the best listener on the planet, and quite talented as well.